THE DEMON'S IN THE DETAILS

MEGHAN MASLOW

The Demon's in the Details

Copyright © 2021 by Meghan Maslow

Cover© 2021 by Alexandria Corza

All rights reserved.

Edited by Lauren Weidner. You can find Lauren at: laurenweidner@counsellor.com

This book is licensed to the original purchaser only. Duplication or distribution via any means is illegal and a violation of international copyright law, subject to criminal prosecution and upon conviction, fines, and/or imprisonment. No part of this book may be reproduced in any form or by any electronic or mechanical means, including information storage and retrieval systems, without written permission from the author, except where permitted by law.

This is a work of fiction. Names, characters, places, and incidents are the product of author imagination, and any resemblance to actual persons, living or dead, business establishments, events, or locales is entirely coincidental.

Sign up for Meghan's newsletter for exclusive content and to learn more about her latest books at **https://www.meghanmaslow.com/**

❀ Created with Vellum

To My Wednesday Crew: **Lauren Weidner**, **Rowan McAllister**, *and* **Venona Keyes**. *Thanks for lifting me up. You all make me a better person.*

1

I, *Poe Dupin, am the greatest jewel thief of my generation.*
That might be a tad bit of an overstatement. Perhaps in Baltimore. In the last 12 hours. On a Thursday. But I was *definitely* the greatest jewel thief during *that* time in *this* city.

It's an accomplishment, don't mock it.

I hoisted myself up the copper-colored skyscraper to the top deck of the former Schaffer Tower—recently renamed Briggs Tower—my job completed. Yes, 1980s architecture at its finest. No point in taking the steps to the spire, though I'd signed my name in black ink at the top some years ago as was tradition for anyone who'd climbed it.

I had the Galdarie diamond—and a few bonus finds—securely in a pouch at my waist. I patted it to make sure, because wouldn't that be embarrassing?

Still there.

My buyer would be ecstatic. Happy client meant a nice bonus. Maybe even repeat business. And next time, a higher price.

It helped ease what little conscience I had that the diamond's previous owner was a first-rate dickbag. A big one. Easy to take from a guy who deserved to have it stolen. And this heist would keep my roost in the black for another month. No, I had no regrets. I was a freaking modern-day Robin Hood. Or Raven Hood as the case may be.

I grinned as I leaned against a flagpole, the replica of the Star Spangled Banner Flag blowing in the breeze. Baltimore at night from almost five hundred feet above street level was a thing of beauty. From up here, the lights shown bright like a private viewing just for me, and making even the most run down areas look festive. The sound of traffic was muted in the night, though a surprising number of cars still motored around the city. The scents from the harbor—salt from the water, grease and chocolate from the food trucks—filled my nose, and I breathed it all in. My city. My home.

But not my Neighborhood. Not yet. Not ever, if I had anything to say about it.

Unlike other cities that have boroughs, districts, or regions, we have Neighborhoods. Five of them officially. And an unofficial sixth. And who leads the Neighborhoods? The Rogers, of course.

Baltimoreans, aka Baltimorons, have a fucked up sense of humor, me included.

But as bad as the Rogers were, I'd rather live in one of their territories than the neutral zone. Talk about survival of the fittest. Being leaderless didn't translate to more freedom, just more desperate people being preyed on.

I took another deep inhale. Fall was often rainy. Tonight the clouds covered the moon but didn't bring rain. Not yet.

Time to go. I was playing with fire. When I strode to the edge of the tower, I held my arms out from my sides.

I leapt off the building.

I whooped. Gravity pulled me toward the ground, wind rushed past my face. I loved the feeling of falling, of flying. My arms became wings, my clothing magically disappeared, and my body transformed into that of a large raven. My whoop became a croak that shouted my freedom and triumph to the winds.

I soared and flew toward home.

"What do you mean, $800,000 by Monday?" I demanded the next morning, my hand slamming down on my jewelry store's glass countertop. "How could you lose that much money? Our roost doesn't *have* that much money."

Ethan Short—my a-hole of a stepdad—grunted. "Just what I said. Briggs Bickley tricked me. We have no choice." He opened the till of my cash register and proceeded to clean out every last dollar. As if that would help.

I raked a hand through hair that was long past due for a trim. Not ready to handle this shit. Friday morning, and I'd only had my first cup of synthetic brew. I needed at least three more before I could process this clusterfuck.

I hadn't even had time to package up the Galdarie diamond for delivery. Last night I'd placed it in my safe, along with a ruby ring, and golden crystal cube with lettering that didn't seem to spell anything but appeased the part of me that liked shiny bits and bobs. Ravens—even raven shifters—weren't much better than magpies. We collected. This score would only bring the roost $175,000. Money for salaries for our community center workers. Now I'd have to donate it to my stepdad's gambling addiction.

Fucking Briggs Bickley. Basilisk shifter. Casino owner. The Roger of Central Baltimore. Bane of my existence. No, wait. That honor went to Ethan. But Briggs was a close second. He kept a chokehold on us ravens so we couldn't prosper. Milked us for protection money. And since he ran the most lucrative areas of Baltimore, which increasingly included our small part of it, we didn't have a choice.

The crook.

Not that I kept my hands all that clean. That's why I owned and ran Spun Gold Jewelers. I was known in Charm City for finding rare gems and magical items for my clientele. Both legally and illegally.

I rounded on my stepdad and stared him down. Ethan was a good three inches shorter and way more than three inches wider. At one time, he'd been quite the bruiser, but in recent years, he'd let himself go.

He was still a mean son-of-a-bitch.

And the roost alpha.

Unlike wolf shifters, a member of the roost couldn't simply challenge their alpha for the position, or I would have done it years ago. The alpha of the roost received magical strength and power from *each* of the members, so no single member could overthrow him or her. You'd be fighting your own strength and that of the rest of the roost.

So no ousting the alpha. And wasn't that just great?

Basically, he'd have to die. While I'd never killed anyone, I considered making an exception for Ethan. The Mid-Atlantic Supernatural Committee wouldn't look fondly on a roost member assassinating their alpha. MASC were a bunch of elitist assholes, anyway. They were more concerned with their power base than helping the little guy.

They weren't what held me back, though.

My half-siblings. Twins. I didn't want to leave them without a parent, even a shitty one. We'd all suffered when my mom died five years ago. Her death changed Ethan from a mediocre alpha to what we had today. Well, that, and I simply wasn't a killer. In self-defense? Sure. But cold-blooded murder? Once I crossed that line, I couldn't cross back.

"You know better than to gamble with Briggs, Ethan. What were you thinking? The kids and families need that money. *We* need that money." I might've loomed over my stepdad, glowering.

Ethan grabbed the front of my black tee and pressed me back against the counter. "You listen to me, boy. You don't speak to me like that. When I married your mama, I let you stay in the roost. Not many alphas would've done so."

While true, Ethan hadn't turned out to be much of an alpha. Not like my dad had been. Why the roost chose him to fill my dad's shoes, I'd never understand. Even less, why my mom had married him afterward.

I didn't cower, but I knew better than to challenge him. Still, I gritted my teeth and said, "You have to get the money back."

I'd never learned to back off. Even to my own detriment.

Ethan laughed. "It's gone. We'll have to make do."

What he meant was *I* would have to make do. In other words, I'd have to up my thieving ways. What started as a way to ensure that our community got much needed resources was now becoming more of a full-time job in order to support Ethan's gambling habit. This was the first time he'd lost such a sum of money to Briggs, though.

Ethan narrowed his eyes when I didn't answer. He slapped my cheek a couple of times and not so gently, either. "You'll need to cover our family's portion of the protection money this month."

I growled. Pretty impressive for a raven shifter if I did say so myself. "What the hell? You gambled that money away, too?"

I'd always had a big mouth. I might be lean, but I still carried honed muscle and wasn't afraid to take a punch.

Good thing, too.

I tensed right before Ethan's fist connected with my midsection. Having the power of the roost behind the blow doubled me over. I dropped to my knees. Before I could draw breath, a kick to the side of my face knocked me to the floor. The crunch my cheekbone made when the boot connected was enough that I let out a pained shout. I could practically see little cartoon stars dancing in front of my eyes.

"You'll cover the expenses. And not give me any more lip if know you what's good for you."

From my position on the floor, I watched Ethan's shiny new cowboy boots retreat. Damn, steel-toed. No wonder my head felt like he'd hit it with a brick.

Don't know how long I lay there when I heard the shop bells tinkle. I watched a pair of teal stilettos—that probably cost more than all the merch in my shop combined—step my way. Those shoes could only belong to . . .

"Poe, are you okay?" Kennedy Fergason sighed, more put out than worried. She knelt next to me, her long chestnut hair brushing my shoulder as she bent to check me over.

Embarrassing much?

Even worse, this wasn't the first time.

"Fine," I croaked, sounding more like a frog than a raven shifter. I knew better than to pick a fight with Ethan after he'd been on a bender. Why my mom had refused to see Ethan's true character remained a mystery to me.

Kennedy tutted, running a hand over my bruised cheek. "You need to shut up around him. He beats on you like a drum. You never seem to learn."

I gingerly sat up. Thanks to shifter healing powers, the

only thing that still hurt was my pride. I gave her my best leer. "Maybe I like having you fuss over me."

"Hon, I'm not your type and you know it." She smirked, rose, then offered me a hand.

I gripped it and pulled myself to my feet.

"What happened?"

I thought about lying. After all, this wasn't her problem, and it was roost business. But Kennedy wasn't just anyone. Sure, she looked like a good Catholic schoolgirl. She wasn't even a shifter. Fully human. She'd grown up in the Roland Park area. Private school, good family, and a wild side that most people missed at a glance. Because of her upbringing, she knew a lot of upstanding members of Baltimore society. And ones not so upstanding in private.

I never figured out why she wanted to work for me, but once she did, she began sending some of those people my way. Before her, I'd only done small-time B&E work. Kennedy encouraged my thieving ways, even helped me find buyers when I lucked across extra pieces in my heists.

What started out as a business relationship quickly turned into a personal one. She started by working in my shop, then inserted herself in my life. Kennedy didn't step softly, either. She conquered. But looking at her perfectly coiffed hair, flawless complexion, and big blue eyes, you'd never know she wore a dagger strapped to her thigh underneath her maxi skirt.

She despised my stepdad almost as much as I did. Plus, she always had good ideas.

So, I told her.

She stayed quiet until I finished, then whistled.

"I can't believe the bastard gambled away 800K," I said, tugging at my hair, the pain grounding. "Who does that?"

"A pretty crummy alpha." Kennedy shook her head. "What are you going to do?"

"I don't know, Kens." I moved from my hair to scratch my 5 o'clock shadowed jaw, even though it was only 9 AM. Some of us were just follicly gifted.

"I knew it!" Kennedy threw up her hands. "You're going to try to fix his mess again."

"Maybe." What was I supposed to do? Ethan didn't even have a job other than roost alpha. Who else was gonna pay this? And if we didn't pay, Briggs would make sure the whole roost paid dearly.

But my measly 175K wasn't even a start.

Where could I come up with $625,000 quickly? That would be a lot of heists, and I didn't currently have a client in the pipeline, much less several. And it's not like I could just decide tomorrow to break in and steal something for somebody. It took planning.

Concentration.

Time.

And therein lay the rub. We didn't have time. Which meant Ethan would start selling off our territory. Or signing it over to Briggs.

Humans didn't have the same notion of territory that shifters did. Territory was *everything*. We only had a couple of blocks. And not prosperous ones. When my dad had been alive and alpha, we'd thrived. At one point, we owned almost eight city blocks. We were down to three. Technically, our blocks fell into Josephine Jones's Neighborhood. Lately, Briggs had been buying the surrounding areas, one building a time. Jones couldn't be happy about it but so far she hadn't come to our aid when Briggs' enforcers started demanding protection money.

It was well known Briggs Bickley wanted the raven

shifters under his thumb. Or at least our streets. He'd already choked out most of the other legitimate businesses in the area. Bail bonds, liquor stores, and pawnshops were the only survivors. Most raven shifters now did odd jobs and found what work they could in the different territories.

If Briggs had his way, we'd be out by the end of the year. Or part of his official Neighborhood, which meant we'd be serving his needs. Not a pleasant thought.

I could approach one of the other four Rogers. But that would just be shifting the debt to a different set of hands. And while Briggs was the worst of the bunch, none of them would get my vote. No loan shark would lend such a huge sum. Not without an astronomical interest rate. Any way I looked at it, I was in a hole and had very few options for digging myself out.

As if following my train of thought, Kennedy tapped a long nail on the counter. "You could go to Tommy Tittoti's place."

I tensed. Everyone knew *about* Tommy. Though he seemed more fairy tale creature than real. Tommy was rumored to be a demon who'd landed in Baltimore a couple hundred years ago. Only a handful of demons remained in the world. Most of them in Europe or Asia. They'd either been driven back through the rift before it had been sealed, or MASC had destroyed them.

But not Tommy.

He somehow made a deal to stay. Some called him an assassin. And that was the nicest name for him. Probably overblown, but this *was* Charm City. One never knew who or what they'd find.

"He demands a price. A high one, I hear."

"He can, but he doesn't always." Kennedy shrugged.

"What do you have to lose? You don't have to accept his bargain."

Bargain? Deal with the devil, more like. Not one of the five Rogers, Tommy owned a small strip of Baltimore that divided several of the territories—kind of like a river meandering through the center. No one, not even Briggs, messed with Tommy.

"How do *you* know him?" I asked. Yeah, I might have been a little suspicious.

Kennedy smiled. "I know a lot of people. That's why I'm telling you to go see him. I think he'll help."

Kennedy had never steered me wrong before. I squinted at her. The picture of innocence.

What kind of bargain would a demon drive anyway?

2

I asked around to find where Tommy Tittoti hung out. Turned out, he owned a barbershop.

Rumpled Still: Skin, Hair, and Scalp.

Not what I was expecting. In fact, I'd rarely had reason to go into Tommy's Neighborhood, except to take in the occasional movie at one of several indie theaters there. The moment I crossed over the green painted line that separated his territory from others, I saw the difference. Clean swept streets, small trees planted along the sidewalks, and all the row housing were new builds, many of them brownstones. Nice.

Now, I stood in front of the old red brick building with the candy-striped barber pole. What was I getting myself into?

Only one way to find out.

Taking a deep breath, I strode inside. The shop crackled with magic, confusing my senses, and raising goosebumps on my skin. I blinked several times trying to adjust, but my sunglasses, I hoped, hid my disorientation. Two large wolf shifters stood beside the doorway. They didn't move when I entered, and it didn't take a genius to tell they were security. They eyed me with distrust but didn't try to stop me.

Four seats near the door made up the waiting area, and while one wall was red brick, the area by the stations was covered in white subway tile. Silver framed mirrors with black cabinetry beneath, and black leather chairs for the clientele, gave a stylish air to the place. Framed black and white posters of Twilight Zone episodes covered the brick wall.

Three barbers worked on clientele. One beast of a creature was tricked out in chains and leather. Bet he had lots of people calling him daddy. Had to be Tommy. A scary dude, for sure, but not as a scary as I'd built him in my imagination. I let out a breath I hadn't realized I'd been holding. I had this.

The other two barbers were . . . odd. At least they didn't look like the types to hang with a demon. An elderly black man wearing jeans and a T-shirt ran clippers over a client's nape. Bald and bearded, the barber was possibly a mage of sorts. Though he didn't smell of magic. Human? The third barber was the hottest little blond twink I'd seen in an age. Mmm. Skinny jeans that hugged a bubble butt, purple Converse, and a form-fitted tee. Another human? Maybe he'd be up for some fun later? I tended to like musclebound guys who could manhandle me, but I wasn't picky. I gave as good as I got.

Tearing my gaze from the twink, I strode to the front desk. A cat shifter with bright pink hair spoke into a cell phone, tapping away on the barbershop's computer keyboard. The name plate on the counter just said "He/Him."

"Yes, that's two weeks from Tuesday at 1:30. Trim and a shave." The cat shifter held up a finger with hot pink polish on the nail and continued with his conversation. When he hung up, he raised a brow as he looked me up and down. He chomped on a stick of gum.

"Well, aren't you the cat's meow? Shouldn't you have a guitar and a couple groupies in tow?"

Yeah, yeah. Black leather, black shades equaled rock star.

I pulled off my shades, placed them on top of my head. "Never heard that one before." Only like a million times. And I didn't even play an instrument unless you counted the skin flute.

"Here for an appointment, hon?" He blew a large bubble.

I drummed my fingers on the reception desk. Now or never. "I want to see Tommy Tittoti."

The bubble popped, and he sucked the gum slowly back into his mouth.

"And I want a fabulous, sparkly diamond ring, dahling. But we don't always get what we want. Unless of course you have an appointment." The guy grinned, like a Cheshire cat.

I gritted my teeth. "I don't. He doesn't take walk-ins?"

The kitty snickered. "First-time client, huh?"

I forced myself to smile and lowered my voice to a sultry purr the cat was bound to appreciate. "That's right."

"Well, he may have something available." The receptionist scrolled through the calendar on the computer and pursed his lips. "Earliest I can fit you in is three weeks from today."

"Can't you see if he's got an opening today?"

"You're smoking hot, babe, but Tommy's got a schedule to keep, and I like my job." The receptionist blew another bubble. I began to turn and caught the luscious little twink nodding at the cat.

"Ooh, looks like someone else thinks you're hot, too. He doesn't usually fit people into his schedule."

While flattering, a tasty twink wasn't the answer to this particular problem. "I told you I need to speak to Tommy."

The cat shifter snickered again. "And which one do you think is Tommy?"

"I assumed—"

"And that was your first mistake, rockstar." He nodded toward the little blond.

"That's Tommy Tittoti?" The disbelief in my voice probably didn't score me any points with the cat.

"Uh-huh." He snapped his gum.

Wow. Tommy had ridiculously long lashes and a mouth meant for sin.

A demon of great reputation? Really?

He didn't look like he could hurt a fly. I didn't know whether to be relieved or even more nervous.

Tommy's long, slender fingers danced as he snipped and fluffed and styled. I hadn't noticed the customer before, but by the time Tommy finished the guy all but oozed sexuality and charm. Were those actual sparkles? That was some kind of magic. What else could the little demon do?

The man stood and thanked Tommy before coming toward the receptionist.

Tommy snapped his fingers, and a broom and dustpan magically swept up the hair. He grabbed a new smock and waved me over.

I gave him my most charming smile, sauntering over with a walk meant to draw the eye. Our gazes met. His eyes suddenly shifted from violet to a fiery red. I stopped in my tracks like I'd run into an invisible wall. Face first. Making eye contact with Tommy Tittoti was a religious experience.

Maybe not the godly kind, though.

My dick hardened, and my breathing sped up. All at

once my skin felt too tight. What kind of demon magic was this?

Tommy practically threw off sparks. His magic hummed around him, making the hair on my arms stand up. How had I missed this amount of sheer power when I'd first seen him? No mistaking it now. And his smell . . . apples. Delicious. Tempting.

Desire shot up from the soles of my feet, radiated throughout every cell until I vibrated with it. Was he an incubus? Had to be. I'd never reacted so strongly to anyone.

The demon's eyes widened for a split second before they returned to violet. He grinned, pointy canines drawing attention to his lack of humanity.

"Have a seat, sugar." His voice dripped with honey.

I blinked. Words. I needed to use them. Right now. Like *right* now. I cleared my throat. Nothing came.

So, I slid into the barber chair. Because I was smooth like that.

Tommy chuckled and wrapped the cape around my neck.

I forced myself to say, "Just a little off the ends—"

"Birdie, you don't need a haircut. Not today." He ran gentle fingers over my scalp, and I swear I could feel the tips of his claws. I'd like to say it terrified me, but my dick was sure on board with what he was doing.

No survival instincts. Much like jumping off a building, I enjoyed the rush.

Tommy removed his hand and retrieved a straight razor and a small bottle.

I tensed. Oh no. No, no, no.

Tommy grinned, his canines definitely looked a little sharper. "What's the matter, sugar? You're not afraid of little ol' me, are you?"

"Should I be?"

"Most definitely." He placed the instruments on a tray, grabbed a machine that sent mist into the air, and angled it toward my face. He stepped behind me. Pushing a lever, he slowly lowered me back, like he was giving me time to refuse.

I gritted my teeth. A shave sounded nice. If my hands gripped the armrest a little tight, well, who could blame me? He picked up a bottle and squirted what looked like thinned-watery shaving cream in his palm.

"Pre-shave oil. Hydrates the skin and softens your bristles." He rubbed his palms together, then placed them on my face. We both jolted, and his eyes flashed red again. He smiled.

I didn't. That was . . . intense. Good thing the cape hid my stiff cock.

He began rubbing the oil into my skin, and my eyes rolled back in my head. Why, oh, why hadn't I ever paid someone to give me a shave before? The scritch of my stubble should have been annoying, but with each pass of his fingertips, I sunk deeper into the chair. When he reached into the warmer to retrieve a steaming towel, I almost whimpered at the loss of his touch. What. The. Everlasting. Fuck.

He wrapped the towel around my jaw, then covered my eyes with the ends. My ears strained to hear exactly where he was moving.

Was I really gonna let him near my throat with a blade?

Tommy moved around, his footsteps loud. Had to be purposeful. A moment later, he unwrapped the towel and applied lather with his hands. He again massaged my face as he worked. He had just finished and grabbed another warm towel when the bell over the door jangled. One of the wolf shifters growled. I angled my neck back to see a pale, middle-aged man enter. He trembled, eyes wide.

"Fee fie foe fum, doesn't look like you fulfilled your part of the bargain, hon." Tommy set the towel on the side table, his gaze focused on the guy with laser intensity. He licked his lips.

Scary and hot all mixed together. I felt his power rise again. I couldn't have moved if someone set the building on fire.

"Tommy, I need a little more time. I can explain—"

"Always with an excuse, Hurst. I warned you what would happen if you didn't follow through. Never make a deal with a demon if you don't intend to pay."

"Please, Tommy. It's not like that."

A large old-fashioned cuckoo clock over the exit struck the hour, and a bird popped out. "Nevermore," it croaked.

"Looks like your time ran out." Tommy shrugged like they were discussing the weather.

"No!" The guy pulled a gun, but Tommy flicked his fingers, and the guy disappeared in a burst of red light. The light then shot into Tommy, and his magic flared and crackled.

A small pile of salt on the floor was all that remained of the guy he'd called Hurst. No sign of the gun. My hands gripped the armrests so tight, they creaked.

Shit, a murder twink. So, maybe I *was* in over my head. MASC might not look so benignly on his doings, but so far they hadn't stopped him. I kept my expression neutral. Damn, what a stark reminder that I dealt with a demon. I swallowed.

Hard.

All noise had ceased, except for the gentle hum of the mist machine. No one dared move.

Tommy sighed. "Michael, clean that up, would you?" He snapped his fingers, and a dustpan and broom sailed over to one of the wolf shifters.

And just like that, everyone resumed their conversations and went back to what they were doing.

Tommy smacked his lips. "At least I don't need lunch now. Okay, sugar, hold still."

He applied a new towel but only for a moment. Next, he dipped a large shaving brush into a container of foam. He liberally applied it in circles until a thick layer coated my neck, jaw, and upper lip. He tilted my chin to the side. Picking up the straight razor, he smirked, then held it next to my skin.

I didn't dare breathe.

Tommy placed the blade against my cheek. He pressed. The straight razor rasped as it moved. My heart thudded. Surprised he couldn't hear it.

Maybe I shouldn't bargain with the devil? Or demon. Whatever.

Still, it couldn't hurt to ask, right? Least I didn't think so. What had Kennedy gotten me into?

I shaved myself in minutes, but Tommy took his time. He ran the blade almost lovingly over every dip. I did my best not to breathe too deeply. After the lather, another towel, more oil, and then more lather. He repeated the process, his touch feeling way better than it had any right to. Damn, a bird could get used to this.

Another towel, and then he held up two bottles, considered them for a heartbeat, and put one back.

"Trust me, sugar, you'll like this one better." He applied a pungent after-shave that made my dick throb. Apples. It smelled of apples. Like him. After-shave? Really? When Tommy finally finished, he raised the chair and held up a hand mirror.

Color me impressed. I normally wore a permanent five o'clock shadow even after a shave. But he'd managed the near impossible feat. For the first time in years, my face was completely hairless.

Not to brag, but I cleaned up pretty well.

"So, birdie, now that I'm done, why don't you tell me why you really came by." Tommy leaned in so we were almost eye to eye.

"How do you know I came for anything but a haircut?"

Tommy sighed. "Because everyone wants something."

Cynic much?

Of course, he was right.

"Fine. I want to know your price to help me clear a debt. An $800,000 debt."

Tommy's leaned away, his eyes glowing that eerie red. "Who do you owe the money to? And how did you lose it in the first place?"

I huffed. As much as I didn't want to tell Tommy roost business, trying to evade his questions might get me turned down. Then again, once I told him, it was unlikely he'd help me anyway. "Briggs Bickley."

Tommy hesitated for a second before going back to rubbing product into my jawline.

Shit. He wasn't gonna do it.

After a moment, Tommy stepped back and leaned against his station. "How do you owe him the money?"

"A game of cards." Keep it simple.

The demon's eyes narrowed. "Who lost the money in a game of cards?"

"Does it matter?"

"Sure does, sugar." He raised a brow and waited.

I thought about lying, but fuck it.

"My stepdad. Ethan Short. He's the roost alpha, so technically he controls the roost's bank account and owns all the property." Well, except my shop and the community center, but that was only because I'd inherited them from my grandma who didn't belong to the roost so he couldn't legally claim them. "Problem is, we don't have that kind of money in our accounts."

I didn't cringe. But I came close. Saying it out loud to a stranger made it worse.

Tommy frowned, a cute furrow appearing between his brows. How weird was it that such a deadly creature looked as harmless as a kitten?

"Briggs cheats."

"Yeah, tell me something I don't know," I snapped. Fucking dumbass Ethan.

Tommy's lips turned up in a hint of a smile. "You're a better man than you let on, sugar."

My reflection in the mirror showed my disbelief. "Sure, whatever."

He pursed his lips. "You ever think of challenging your alpha? It'd be simpler than taking on Briggs."

"We're not like wolves. We can't challenge our alpha."

He nodded, like he understood. Maybe he did.

"Well then, sugar, there's a much simpler option than dealing with me." He drew a finger across his neck, a wicked-looking claw appearing for emphasis.

He wasn't playing around. "Yeah, but there's my half-siblings to consider. They're only nine."

Tommy shrugged. "Shifters always take the hard road."

"Even if I did as you say, we'd still owe the money. My stepdad's markers are ours. Can you help me or not?" I didn't growl. But I came close. I wasn't truly upset with him. I was just so frustrated with the situation. I didn't like having to ask *anyone* for *anything*, much less a demon. But what choice did I have?

"I can do lots of things. The question is whether you're willing to pay my price, Poe Dupin." Tommy tilted my chin up and examined his handiwork.

His fingertips burned, but in a pleasurable way, and sent sparks zinging to my dick. Made it hard to concentrate. Probably the demon's plan.

Wait. I tensed. "How'd you know my name?"

Tommy laughed, like the tinkling of bells. It warmed my chest against my will. Fucking demon magic.

"I know a lot of things, birdie. Nature of the beast."

The reminder of his nature took the warmth away. Right. Demon. Not to be trusted. "What's the price?"

Tommy ran a finger down my cheek. "For you? Nothing much. I want your sunglasses. They're Enigmas, right?"

My mouth fell open. WTF? Kennedy had bought the overpriced shades for my birthday last year. Still, four hundred dollars hardly equaled the 800k I needed. "You're willing to give me eight-hundred thousand for my sunglasses?"

Yeah, I sounded disbelieving.

Tommy grinned, not seeming at all offended. "That, and I want access to your community center for my Neighborhood on Sundays. You can still have your people there, but mine also can come in for free."

What in the hell kind of bargain was that? "Why? You have a much larger and nicer one. I passed it on the way in."

"Take it or leave it, sugar. That's my price."

The demon's voice resonated on the last word. It sent a chill racing through my body. I sat up straighter in the barber's chair. How did he know I could make that deal? I didn't exactly advertise that I owned the space. My skin tingled. "What's the catch?"

"I'm not going to force you to take my deal. I've told you I want your sunglasses and access to your community center one day a week. If you don't want the money, just get up and leave."

"You got yourself a deal," I blurted before I could think better of it. One day, I'd learn to think before I spoke. Today was not that day.

Tommy nodded, and a small clap of thunder sounded within the shop.

I looked around expecting things to be different in some way. Nothing happened. "When do I get the money?"

"Come back tomorrow afternoon with a handful of your shop's costume jewelry, and I'll have it for you."

Costume jewelry? How did he know I owned a cheap-end jewelry shop? Instead, I asked, "Why would you need that old junky stuff?"

"You'll see."

"Why not now?"

"Patience, Poe. A demon's got other priorities, and"—he looked to the door as a young human came in—"other clients."

I pulled the sunglasses from my hair and tried to hand them to him.

He waved me away. "You can give them to me tomorrow."

Nuh-uh. I wasn't leaving the shop with the sunglasses. If something happened to them, I would be in breach of our bargain. I'd already seen what happened to someone when they didn't pay up.

"I'd rather you take them now."

Tommy raised a brow. He didn't smile, but he was clearly amused. "Not a very trusting creature, are you, sugar?"

"Nope."

"I like you better and better." He held out his hand, and I transferred the glasses to him. Our fingers brushed, and I felt that strange electricity again. If he felt it, he didn't let on. He slid them on his nose and damn if they didn't look fucking scorching on him. Way too hot not to be magical. He removed the cape from around my neck and pointed me back toward reception.

I glanced in the mirror again and gaped. I looked . . . fantastic. And I wasn't a slouch before. I paid the cat shifter and left a nice tip. I knew better than to cheap out.

Now, if only the demon would follow through.

3

"You want me to work on the front display now?" Oliver Clemm said the next morning. He'd placed some of the new items within locked glass cases. Though young, the raven shifter had a good eye for quality. His grandfather had been one of the original jewelers in this part of town. Seemed he inherited those qualities from his family.

Ollie also had a record. Not too surprising for a raven, since we tended to be collectors of both legal and illegal things. But Ollie had stolen a car in a high school joyride with some human "friends". They got busted in Bickley's Neighborhood. While it hadn't been Ollie's idea, the others all blamed him and claimed he'd been the driver.

He hadn't.

But Briggs didn't care. Those kids came from wealthy human families. Patrons. Like the rest of the ravens, Ollie's family had fallen on hard times. No money. No pull. So he'd been shipped to juvie for eighteen months, and when he got out, he found that nobody wanted to hire him.

So, I gave him a shot.

I grunted. I'd been out of sorts since leaving Tommy's shop yesterday afternoon. Afterward, I'd arranged and met with my client to exchange the diamond for the 175K. Put it in a private account that my stepdad couldn't access. Not that it would last long, if Ethan kept gambling the way he did.

I'd slept poorly, worrying about the deal I'd made. Too easy. Had to be a trap, right? But how? I fulfilled my part of the bargain. It was up to him to fulfill his. And if Tommy didn't, then I was out an expensive pair of sunglasses—and a little bit more of my pride. But I couldn't see a way he could turn this on me.

And that freaked me out. What didn't I see?

To add insult to injury, when I finally fell asleep last night, I'd had strange, erotic dreams about Tommy. Was he in my head? Or was it simply my vivid imagination? My vivid, *horny* imagination. He *had* to be an incubus. I should've asked. Or was that rude? I didn't know proper demon etiquette.

After the string of erotic dreams left me sexually frustrated, I'd given up and gone for a run early this morning. Exercise hadn't helped my mood. I was still horny as fuck. Even a quick jerk-off session hadn't dulled that particular ache.

Sure, Tommy was my type. Then again, so were a lot of others. And I didn't dream about them in such lurid detail.

Screw that demon.

If Tommy managed to get the 800K, I'd thank him and never see him again. I didn't need more problems.

I wasn't exactly afraid of him, but I had a healthy respect for staying alive. As harmless and angelic as he looked on the surface, his lack of remorse for killing a man was a stark reminder of his true nature.

And that nature was *dark*.

Wrapped up in a frustratingly sexy murder twink package. But still dark as hell.

"Poe, you gonna answer me?"

"Huh? Oh, sorry, Ollie. Zoned out. What'd you say?" I ran a hand over my slightly stubbled jaw. The smooth shave didn't last long, but I'd found myself touching my face without thought all morning.

"Do you have a problem if I redesign the front window? It needs a refresher."

"You sound like Kens. Oh, dahling, give it a little refresher," I said in my snootiest accent. I didn't dare risk selling the stolen ruby ring in my shop or that weird crystal cube. I'd ask Kennedy to find a buyer for the ring but wasn't sure what to do about the cube. For now, I'd just leave it in the safe.

"I'm taking that as a compliment." Ollie kept looking at me from under long lashes. The kid was jumpy at the best of times. Being small and ridiculously cute wouldn't have made his time in juvie easy.

I leaned on the counter, shined up an amethyst ring I'd acquired last week. "What's up, Ollie? You've clearly got something on your mind."

The kid winced and bit his bottom lip. He'd recently shaved the sides of his thick, tightly curled hair and left it long on top. It emphasized his heart-shaped face, though it made him seem even younger than his eighteen years. He looked like he should be riding a skateboard and wearing ripped jeans and a tee that said, "Skate or Die." Instead, he wore a white button-down and loose-fitting khaki slacks. Since I didn't keep a dress code, this turned out to be Ollie's style choice.

I let the kid stew as I polished another ring and put it back in its setting. When I looked up, Ollie still had a pensive look on his face.

"What? Go on, spit it out."

He swallowed. "I don't mean any disrespect, Poe. But

word spreads fast through the roost. What if . . . what if our alpha keeps doing this? We can't pay as it is. Heard my mom say some of us might have to sell our homes to cover the debt."

"I've got it covered." No one was losing their home on my watch. Not if I could help it.

Ollie's eyes narrowed. "How're you planning to do that?"

"Doesn't matter." It's not that I wanted to hide Tommy per se, but dealing with a demon would freak the rest of my roost out. The fewer who knew the better.

"You keep bailing him out."

I grumbled. "Yeah."

"Maybe . . . You shouldn't."

Before I could think more on it, a Hummer with a custom paint job skidded to a halt in front of my shop. Snake scales. I didn't know whether to be grossed out or impressed. Maybe a bit of both.

Andre, one of Briggs' favorite enforcers—a mean-ass boar shifter—hopped out of the passenger seat, then came around and held open the back door. Holy shit. Briggs Bickley himself slithered out.

Okay, he didn't really slither, but the imagery fit. Why the hell was he visiting my shop?

"Ollie—" I began.

"I know. Go to the back." His voice had gone up an octave. He raced through the curtain and disappeared.

Didn't have to ask him twice. One less worry.

The bell over my shop tinkled, and Briggs entered, dwarfed by Andre's brutish form.

"Good morning, Poe Dupin." Briggs smiled, his teeth artificially whitened, his bespoke suit showing off his lanky frame. His pate had been freshly oiled and gleamed under the shop's lights.

How the hell did he know my name? First Tommy, now him.

"Seems you wanted my attention. And now you've got it." Briggs sauntered my way.

Andre threw the bolt on the front door.

Glad I had the store's front counter between us.

"I'm sorry, Mr. Bickley, have we met?" I didn't smile back.

"Met? No. But you came into my Neighborhood and took property that didn't belong to you."

The hair on the nape of my neck prickled. Had there been a camera I hadn't been aware of? No, I'd been careful. Really careful. Though my reputation may have preceded me. Still, plausible deniability.

"I'm not sure what you mean." I forced myself to add, "Sir."

"You know, Poe, you're a good liar. If I didn't know that you'd entered my property, I might even believe you. But you took something. Something that belonged to a friend of mine that I was taking care of for him." Bickley stuffed his hands in his pockets. "*That* is unacceptable."

I swallowed. "Respectfully, Mr. Bickley, you've got the wrong bird."

"So you didn't steal the Galdarie diamond for Kiros Assefa?" Bickley plucked the gem from a pocket, held it up.

Oh shit. I froze.

Bickley smiled, tucked the diamond back in his pocket. "Your friend had an unfortunate accident. I'm sure you'll read about it in tomorrow's paper. So clumsy. Falling from the roof of a building."

I swallowed. "That's too bad."

He tsked. "Good thing we had a little chat before he left this Earth."

I had nowhere to run, and even if I flew away, it would

only be a matter of time before I was back in Briggs Bickley's sight. "What do you want?"

"You know, Poe, you're very talented. I thought my vault was thief-proof. You proved me wrong. I don't like to be wrong."

I braced for a fight. I wasn't going down without one.

Briggs chuckled. "Oh, don't worry. I'm not planning to hurt you. In a way, I guess you could say, I'm offering you a job."

"A job?" I didn't relax because that would be the signal for the snake to strike.

"Of sorts. I'd like you to work for me exclusively. I consider myself a visionary. I see things others don't. And I see you. With your talents you could go far. Plus, I have some items I'd like you to retrieve."

Visionary? Ugh. "I'm sure we can make a deal, Mr. Bickley."

He grinned, and I swear his tongue was forked. "I don't doubt that. But unfortunately I can't let your transgression go unanswered."

"Meaning?" My fists clenched behind the counter.

"Once you accept my proposition, I will *own* you. You will only work for me. You will be at my beck and call. And you will serve me in any way I desire. And Poe, I have to say seeing you in person, I have lots of desires."

What the fuck? "I'm certainly willing to work for you, sir. But I'm my own bird. Always have been, always will be."

Andre grunted from his position against the front door.

"It's cute that you think so. And I did say I wouldn't *physically* hurt you. I'm a man of my word. But also a sporting man. So I'm giving you until Monday evening to come up with the $900,000 that your dad—"

"$800,000. And he's my step-dad."

"—owes me. 900. There's interest now." He patted his pocket. "You get that to me on Monday, you're off the hook." Briggs eyes remained unblinking, his gaze predatory.

He seemed sure I wouldn't be able to come up with the cash.

"And Poe, when you fail, be prepared to grovel. I think you'll look good on your knees."

I was a quick tumble in the back alley kind of bird, not some fancy peacock. But that didn't mean I didn't have standards. Even if they were low ones.

Not *that* low.

Briggs went unnaturally still, and Andre, his overgrown lapdog, snarled.

Great. My expression must've shown my distaste. So much for a poker face. There was a reason *I* didn't play cards.

"Most people in this town would kill for such an honor." Briggs swayed forward a little, leaning over the counter and into my space. His eyes lit up an ominous yellow, before returning to their shrewd brown.

I quickly looked away. He'd turned more than one creature who displeased him to stone. He ran the back of a knuckle across my cheek. It took everything I had not to punch his lights out. I didn't doubt I'd find myself in a shallow grave or part of his statuary collection. He didn't bluff.

"That's what I thought. Pack an overnight bag. You'll need it."

Briggs nodded to Andre, who unlocked and held the door for him. Andre shot me a smirk over his shoulder as they departed. Bastard.

Ollie peeked out from the back room. "Safe for me to come out?"

"Yeah, he's gone." I took a ragged breath.

"Wow. What are you going to do?"

My hands gripped the counter so tightly that my knuckles turned white. I closed my eyes and took a few shallow breaths. Kiros had been pretty much untouchable. Or so I'd thought.

Now I was on Briggs Bickley's radar. Not good. Not good at all.

"What are you going to do, Poe?" Ollie repeated. He looked as scared as I felt.

"I don't know, kid. But I'll think of something." Even if I came up with the money, would I really be off the hook?

4

I strode into Rumpled Still in the late afternoon on Saturday with a handful of junk jewelry. Cheap costume stuff that I often sold at local events like Hon Fest. I didn't see Tommy anywhere. The cat shifter stood behind the desk and smirked when he noticed me. For some reason, it raised my hackles.

"Back so soon, rockstar?"

"Do all cats flirt so outrageously on the job?" I couldn't help but ask.

"Only when we're awake."

I chuckled in spite of myself. Such a cat. "Tommy around?"

"He's on break. You can go on back. He's expecting you."

That didn't sound ominous or anything. I huffed out an annoyed breath. Best to get it over with. I marched toward the direction the cat pointed. I strode through a door and found myself in a corridor with rooms on each side, only one with the door open. I headed straight for it.

Tommy sat curled up in a teal overstuffed chair, a steaming cup of coffee in his hands. He'd removed his Converse and pulled on a pair of monster feet slippers. Funny guy. He smiled over the rim of the cup when I walked in.

I meant to get right down to business, but seeing the

little demon looking so cute and harmless unnerved me for a moment. It also shot a bolt of lust to my belly. Damn demon magic. Least I was on to him.

"Cat got your tongue?" Tommy continued to smile. He gave me a thorough once-over. While the cat shifter's flirting hadn't done anything for me, it had seemed harmless enough. But Tommy's gaze was anything but harmless. Hungry, more like. I felt that same hunger, though I kept expecting my survival instinct to kick in at any time and remind me that Tommy was a demon with a capital D.

It didn't.

"Do you have the 800K?" My voice came out unsteady. So much rode on his answer.

"So eager to be done with our bargain?" Tommy broke eye contact and took a long sip of coffee. "Ah, nectar of the gods."

One thing we agreed on. Though Tommy could probably afford a much higher quality bean than the synthetic crap found in my neck of the woods.

"You didn't answer my question."

"No, I didn't." Tommy finished his coffee and set the mug down. "I'm giving this to you as almost a freebie. I've a reputation to uphold, so don't spread it around too far." He held out his hands for the jewelry.

I handed it over.

"Ooh, nice and tacky." He focused on the pile, and with a flash of light, gold replaced the jewelry.

An erect gold phallus to be exact.

"What is..."

"Do I need to explain the birds and the bees, sugar?" Tommy held it out, and I reached for it. He pulled it back. "A demon likes to be thanked for his hard work."

I attempted to smile, but it probably came out more like a grimace. "If it's real gold, then thank you."

"If? Now, birdie, that's insulting. Of course it's real gold. You're the *jeweler*. You should know better." Tommy snickered but held out the gold phallus again.

I lunged forward and snatched it from his hand. Damn, it was heavy. Had to weigh at least 30 pounds. I placed it under my nose and drew in a deep breath. Humans had no clue, but precious metals and even gems had particular scent signatures. This was definitely solid gold. "That's some magic you've got there."

"We demons have our uses." This time a dimple appeared, making him look even more angelic. Then he tilted his head and sniffed.

So I did, too. Solid gold, like I'd said.

His eyes turned red, and his fangs dropped.

What the . . . I took a quick step away, but his hand lashed out and snagged my wrist. He yanked me onto his lap before I could even think to resist. He sniffed again. "Why did Briggs Bickley touch you, sugar?" His voice rumbled like the clouds before a storm.

"He didn't." I struggled weakly, but he kept me exactly where he wanted me, his eyes burning brighter, his claws digging into my wrist. And why I didn't pound him with the gold phallus, I couldn't say. But my skin tingled, and the enticing smell of apples made me lightheaded. I had the sudden strange urge to curl into him.

"I can smell him on you." His lip curled.

"He touched my cheek." I swallowed.

"Why?"

Trick question? What did he want me to say? I stared into his eyes.

"He wants me to work for him." Damn, I hadn't considered I'd tell the truth.

"But *why* did he put his hands on you?" Tommy's voice came out garbled through his fangs.

"Because he caught me stealing from him. And now he wants retribution. My ass, for one. An extra 100K added to my stepdad's debt. If I don't pay it . . ." I shrugged. It wasn't his problem.

His eyes flared bright, then abruptly returned to a placid purple. "Why didn't you say so, birdie?"

He pried the golden phallus from my hand and released me.

I scrambled to my feet.

"What are you doing?" I needed that gold.

"Patience, Poe." Tommy stroked the phallus from tip to base a couple of times. He had the wrist action down. The phallus seemed to swell. "That should do it."

When he handed it back, I could feel the added weight. He'd given me the extra 100K. I shouldn't look a gift demon in the mouth, but why would he do such a thing?

"I don't suppose there's any possibility that you would consider changing the shape?" Okay, yeah, *that's* what came out of my mouth. But Tommy didn't seem mad.

"Oh no, sugar. Look at this as my calling card." Tommy grinned, his fangs now retracted.

"Briggs is gonna be . . . upset if I give him this."

"He's going to be upset anyway. He doesn't want you to pay. Besides, this won't be the first time someone has showed up with a golden phallus for him. Trust me."

Ha! Not on my life. But I did remember my manners. "Thank you for this. I don't know what kind of bargains you usually make, but I appreciate what you've done for my roost."

The smile slipped from Tommy's face. "I didn't do this

for your roost, Poe. I did this for *you*. I only bargain with individuals." The look he gave me was so intense I had to fight taking a step back. What he was telling me was important, but I couldn't be sure why.

"Then I appreciate what you did for me."

He nodded. "Listen, sugar, you should work on getting a new roost. Your stepdad is irresponsible. He'll just get you into more trouble. Take it from a guy who's been around the block a time or 200."

I tucked the phallus into my old, beat up backpack. Knowing my luck, I'd be jumped on the way home. I met his eyes for a brief second. "It's complicated."

As I turned to go, Tommy called after me, "It always is, sugar."

∼

I swore I would stay away from the community center on Sunday. Yet here I stood the next morning leaning against an outside wall, waiting to see if any of Tommy's people showed up. It had nothing to do with Tommy. Nope. Not a damn thing.

"Fuck this," Ethan spat. "Why would you let outsiders use our facilities, dumbass?"

Yes, we were a close-knit family. I grimaced.

"Because it was the only way I could get the money for Briggs." I itched to punch Ethan in his ungrateful face. Instead of being thrilled that I had managed to get my hands on enough gold to pay off our debt, he'd been bitching for the last hour about how I'd fucked up. He also blew a gasket when I informed him I wouldn't be showing him the money. I didn't trust that he wouldn't gamble it away. That went over like a lead balloon.

A skinny lone wolf, a bunch of humans, and the cat shifter from the barbershop strolled toward the door of the community center.

"Bunch of losers." Ethan moved to intercept them, but I grabbed his arm.

"Listen, this is what I had to do to get *your* debt repaid. The least you can do is be nice to them. If you hadn't fucked up, this wouldn't be necessary."

"I told you to watch your tone, boy." Ethan slammed me against the community center wall.

I hit hard enough to rattle my teeth. My head throbbed where it smacked the brick.

"I'm not a boy." I tried to shove Ethan away, but he drew on the strength of the roost and kept me immobile. He grabbed the front of my T-shirt and slammed me against the wall again. At this rate, I'd have a concussion in no time.

"Poe!" two small voices chimed in together. The twins. Lucy and Jamie.

Ethan released his grip on my shirt and smoothed his hand over my chest. He stepped back just as the twins barreled into me. I caught them both in a hug. Hard to believe they were nine already.

Lucy wore her dark hair in pigtails. Her tee had a unicorn on it, and she wore a sparkly tutu and rainbow knee socks. Jamie had recently asked me to cut his hair into a fauxhawk, and he wore mismatched socks with navy trackpants that were a little too short. I'd need to get him a longer pair. His tee wasn't much better. When did he get so tall?

"Hey, munchkins. Coming to the center?"

"We wanted to play dodgeball," Lucy grinned. The girl could throw harder than most grown men. If you were smart, you put her on your team.

I slid away from my stepdad and gripped the twins'

hands. I looked back over my shoulder, and Ethan gave me a look that could melt the pavement. Yeah, we'd be discussing this again later.

"I'll keep them for the day, if you're busy," I offered. It might smooth his feathers a bit since he wouldn't have to look after them. Then again, he didn't do much of that now.

He tilted his chin in acknowledgement, then turned away from us and Tommy's people. He didn't look back.

I moved to the front doors to greet the strangers.

"Hey, rockstar. I figured you'd be here," the cat shifter said. "I'm Carter Strike, by the way."

It took everything I had not to ask whether Tommy would be making an appearance. The only reason I wanted to know was so that I could avoid seeing him. Or that's what I told myself anyway. Self-deception wasn't always a bad thing.

I introduced myself and my half-siblings. Jamie eyed the wolf with interest. "You any good at dodgeball?" he asked.

The wolf seemed startled that he was being addressed. He stuffed his hands in his pockets. "Used to be good. Haven't played in a while."

Jamie's eyes lit up. "Cool. You can play on my team." He leaned toward the wolf and lowered his voice. "My sister's a shark. You gotta watch out for her."

The wolf glanced at Lucy and raised an eyebrow. I didn't laugh, but it was a close call. Oh, she was so gonna school him.

Carter looked between the wolf and my sister. "I'm on her team."

"Smart move." I waved them inside and followed.

Maybe this would work out after all.

5

A day later, I found myself having dinner with Briggs Bickley and my stepdad in the VIP suite at the Snake Eyes Casino. Everything was decorated in red and black and the tables looked like giant poker chips. So did the drink coasters. We sat in stiff, red leather chairs with black legs. Cigar smoke and Briggs' cologne scented the air. Between the odors and the dim lighting, my head started to throb.

Briggs scowled. This was definitely not what he expected. Ethan refused to look him in the eye and cowered in his seat.

The golden phallus sat on the table between us. Briggs did *not* look amused. I made sure not to laugh, though keeping a straight face proved more difficult than I would have thought with a basilisk giving me the stink eye.

"How do you know Tommy Tittoti?" Briggs leaned back in his seat, his eyelids unblinking, his hands linked together on his belly like he wasn't bothered by a gold erect phallus in the middle of his table.

"He's the one who knows him." Ethan pointed at me with his thumb.

Way to throw me under the bus. Not that I expected anything better from Ethan Short.

Instead, I tried to look relaxed, too, though all my

instincts were on high alert. "I met him the other day. Cool guy."

Briggs continued to stare at me. Finally, he nodded. "Just the other day? Or do you do *business* with him?"

"No, I met him the other day. As I said."

"You have a smart mouth, Poe. Sass won't keep you alive long in my Neighborhood. Whether you like it or not, this only delays the inevitable."

And it galled me that he was more than likely right. I hoped Ethan was listening closely and would snap to his senses. He needed to stay away from the casinos—and certainly from Briggs Bickley.

Briggs waved a waiter away who arrived with a bottle of wine. "I think we'll postpone our dinner for another time. I'm a patient man. As I said before, a visionary. I enjoy taking things away. One by one. Until there are no options left." He stared at me the whole time he said this. Like Ethan wasn't even there. "Remember, the longer you make me wait for what I want, the more I'll glory in owning it later."

While I knew he spoke of our territory more generally, he also made it abundantly clear as his eyes roved over my body that I was his possession. Or soon would be. Felt like being dipped in grease. I didn't shudder, but it was close.

"Andre, show Mr. Dupin and Mr. Short out."

Ethan shot to his feet and all but ran for the exit. I tried to play it cool, though there was a little pep to my step, too. Couldn't wait to get away from Briggs.

Ugh, now I needed a shower.

Maybe some bleach.

Andre sniggered as he followed us a moment later to the VIP elevator. He used his card, and the door slid open. We all entered.

No one said anything as the elevator descended, but

when the doors opened, Andre pulled out a handful of casino chips and handed them to Ethan. "Mr. Bickley appreciates you paying your debt. To show his ongoing friendship, he'd like to give you a few of these tokens to spend in the casino this evening."

Ethan's eyes grew wide. Five tokens each worth 1K. He licked his lips. "Thank Mr. Bickley for me. He's always been so good to the ravens."

"Speak for yourself," I grumbled.

Andre shoved me into the wall, and I bounced. He plowed into me and placed his meaty forearm across my throat. "You don't talk about Mr. Bickley like that. I'm going to enjoy watching him take you apart piece by piece. You're an egotistical little shit. You think because you have a cute ass, you're worth something. You're not."

I would have told him to fuck off, but there was that whole thing about not being able to breathe. When he still didn't let go, I raised my knee and rammed it into his groin. He dropped like a stone.

Ah, that's better. I adjusted my leather jacket, stepped around him, and went to grab Ethan.

Fuck. He'd disappeared. That weak-assed bastard.

Andre rolled to his knees, still grasping his crotch. "I'm going to fucking kill you."

"Is that any way to talk to your boss's boyfriend?" I quipped.

He growled, and I made a hasty retreat.

Paying the money seemed to have only increased the debt.

~

Banging on my shop's glass door woke me the next morning. I'd come home from my meeting with Briggs and picked up the twins for the night, relieving their babysitter. They slept in bunkbeds at the back of my shop. I'd been living in the back room since my mom died. It wasn't much, but it had beds, a hotplate, small fridge, and I'd installed a full bathroom. I never stayed in Ethan's house anymore. Wasn't allowed to even if I were so inclined.

I wasn't.

After the twins went to bed, I sat in the front of the shop and imbibed a couple Natty Bohs. Just needed to take the edge off the day. My meeting with Briggs shook me up more than I wanted to admit. I'd polished some of the jewelry, and shined up the crystal cube before returning it to the safe. I needed to remember to ask Kennedy what she thought I should do with it, as well as the ruby ring.

The banging continued, so I glanced at my phone. 6:30 AM. Tuesday. My day off. Damn. This better be important. Kennedy wasn't due in for another hour and a half yet.

I scrubbed at my sleep-crusted lids and stumbled out of bed wearing boxer briefs. I snatched up a pair of pajama pants that I'd left crumpled by the side of the bed. I almost tripped trying to get them on, then made my way on unsteady feet to the door, phone in hand.

Abraham Williams, one of Ethan's betas, raised his fist to knock again before seeing me and lowering it.

After undoing the locks and disabling the alarm, I yanked the door open. "What the hell, Abe—"

"What happened last night, Poe?" Abe brushed past me. "Weren't you supposed to pay off Briggs?"

"Shhh, the kids are sleeping." I glared at him, keeping my voice low. "I did. He wasn't happy, but he accepted the payment."

"Wasn't Alpha with you?" Abe whispered back, his brows drawn low, a hand raking through his graying locs.

Alpha? I snorted. "Yeah, Ethan was there. For all the good he was."

"Don't joke, Poe. We're fucked."

I rubbed my eyes, trying to wake up. I sighed. I needed coffee. "What happened?"

"Alpha killed a man. One of Briggs' men. Now Briggs is demanding a blood sacrifice. A life for a life." Abe pursed his lips, rubbed at his goatee.

Oh, wow. I pressed on my forehead.

"That sounds like Ethan. Asshole." Briggs had the right to claim the sacrifice if my stepdad had really done as claimed. His Neighborhood. He got to keep the peace.

"Poe, this is serious! Briggs won't let me see Alpha. Said he wants to talk to you. *Only* you. What's going on? Why would he want to see *you*?"

I groaned. Did Briggs think I'd bargain for my stepdad's life? That had to be it. A roost needed an alpha. *Buuut* . . . if the alpha were killed . . .

Tommy's words came back to me. *Well then, sugar, there's a much simpler option than dealing with me.*

Abe might be semi-loyal to the loser, but the roost was better off without Ethan. Even Abe had to see that. We had some strong betas. Several would make decent alphas. Including Abe. Not that we had super high standards at this point.

I had no intention of bargaining for Ethan's miserable life. Not in good faith, anyway. Lucy and Jamie came to mind. A twinge. But Ethan wasn't much of a father to them, and I'd make sure to be present in their lives. Hell, I did all the dad things anyway—went to their school events, their games, took them to the community center on the week-ends. I'd kept my promise to my mom as best I could. Ethan now made that impossible. A huge weight lifted from my shoulders.

Briggs was doing us a favor.

He just didn't know it.

I swallowed. I'd have to play this one carefully.

"Did he say when he wants to meet?" I asked.

Before Abe could answer, my phone beeped.

A message.

See you in two hours. Don't be late.

An address followed. Hands shaking from both excitement and nerves, I set my phone down on the counter.

I had a roost to save.

6

Luckily, I'd pulled myself together and gotten the kids ready for school. Kennedy had agreed to get them there.

I arrived at the Brigadeiro with five minutes to spare. The Brazilian diner sat on 'Charm-tastic' Mile, firmly in Briggs' Neighborhood. The restaurant had a well-shaded outdoor patio and the best brunch this side of Baltimore. Way out of my price range, but that was par for the course.

I took a calming breath. No way was I trading anything for Ethan's life. Not even a five-dollar bill. He'd done enough damage already. I'd have to figure out a way to talk to the twins, but that was a later-problem and I had a now-problem. A big one.

I'd hidden my hair under a beanie and purposely wore a pair of scuffed jeans and an old worn-in tee and my trusty jacket and boots. I wasn't doing anything to impress Briggs. He wouldn't expect it, anyway. My palms felt damp, and my stomach ached. I'd never be able to eat.

The maître d' clearly expected me and led me to a canopied table at the back of the patio. Lush vines ringed the table, honeysuckle still blooming even this late in the season.

There Briggs lounged like a king, sipping a flute of caipirinha, his entourage scattered around other tables.

Andre stood at his shoulder, looking oh-so-smug. The dick grinned as I approached. But I couldn't bother to flip him off, especially since he was only a lackey.

I needed to stay focused on the real threat.

Briggs waved me to a chair across from him, his eyes gleaming, but his expression giving little away. "Ah, Poe, so good to see you again. I admit, I thought it would be a little longer, but events happen in mysterious ways."

Mysterious? I doubted it. Instead I sank into the chair and picked up the menu. "What's good here?"

His lids slowly lowered in a blink. "I've ordered for you."

That fucker. "Great. Saves me the trouble." I couldn't make myself smile, but I was determined not to play his games.

"You'll get used to it."

Fuck you. "I bet you say that to all the boys." I poured myself a cup of coffee from a large carafe and took a sip. Divine. The real stuff.

He tilted his head to the side in a pose that was so snake-like it curdled the coffee in my mouth. I set my mug down. Nope. Not gonna be able to eat.

We sat in silence, neither of us moving.

When he leaned back, I almost gasped in relief. Not that I'd show him that.

"Aren't you going to ask about your dad?"

"Step. I mean, yes, of course." I schooled my features, tried to make myself seem concerned. "How is he?"

Too much?

Briggs laughed. Came out as a hiss. "I like you, Poe. You're going to be so much fun."

That didn't sound so good. "I wasn't really going for amusement, but hey, I'm a funny guy."

Before Briggs could answer, three wait staff arrived with

trays of food. A server placed a plate of crab benedict with a healthy sprinkling of Old Bay before me, while Briggs had most of the rest. Plates were set on the other tables as well.

Though I hated that he ordered for me, I made myself slowly cut up the meal. Wasn't hungry. Could barely manage the thought of eating. Besides, I was pretty sure crab benedict wasn't a Brazilian specialty, though it came on cheesy bread instead of English muffins.

He didn't seem to have a problem with his appetite. At. All. Much like a snake, he placed large amounts of food in his mouth and slowly swallowed without chewing. Unnerving? Oh, yeah.

I pushed my food around on my plate a bit, managed to take a single bite. While the benedict was melt-in-your-mouth delicious, it might as well have been made of ash.

We ate in silence. It wasn't uncomfortable or anything. Nah.

When Briggs finally placed his fork down, I stopped all pretense of eating and set my silverware down as well. He used a napkin and wiped off his mouth, taking his own sweet time. Being powerless sucked. But I dealt with lots of rich assholes in my jewelry heists, so I was pretty good at pretending it didn't bother me.

"You must wonder why I asked you here."

"I assumed you wanted to bargain for Ethan's life."

Another hiss. God, I hated that laugh.

"What would you have to bargain with?" Briggs raised a thin brow. "No, if I were to bargain, it would be because I *needed* something. But I hold the winning hand. So no, there will be no bargaining."

I could feel the muscle in my jaw tick. "Then why did you invite me here?"

I figured this was the part of the villain's monologue

where he'd say he wasn't gonna bargain, he was gonna demand. Fucker.

"I want you to make a choice, of course."

He sounded a little too smug. The hair on my nape raised.

"What kind of choice?" I ran my finger around the rim of the coffee mug.

"Well, seeing as Ethan is your roost's alpha, I'd hate to leave the roost in such chaos. And I'm a very reasonable man. Ethan did a terrible, terrible thing. But I'm inclined to spare his life."

"Uh-huh?" I drew in a deep breath through my nose, trying to keep my posture relaxed. If this was the part where he said I had to be a sacrificial lamb, or raven as the case may be, I had news for him. I was done saving Ethan Short from disasters of his own making.

"Don't you think that's kind of me, Poe?" he leaned forward, and I swear it was like a snake preparing to strike. All my instincts were telling me to run. But I couldn't do that. Not yet.

"Sure, sugar and spice and everything nice."

He grinned. "And that's why I'm choosing to spare him."

"But you mentioned a choice?"

"Of course. The blood debt has to be settled."

I blinked. Oh. Did he actually think I'd give up my life for that fucker? Was that what he was asking? I'd thought . . .

He hissed again. "No, silly bird, not you. I have some lovely *plans* for you."

I narrowed my eyes. What game was he playing at?

"I don't understand."

"As is my right, I claim blood for blood. I gave your father a choice. His life or one of his blood. Even if I'd wanted it to be you, you're not of his blood. But I understand you have two younger siblings—"

I sprung up almost toppling the table. I bared my teeth. "No! You have no right. They're children."

"Your dad didn't have any problem with trading his life for one of theirs." Briggs snapped his fingers, and Andre pulled out a contract signed in blood. He held it up, and even from where I stood, I could see the magic swirling around it.

Son of a bitch.

"You can't be serious." But I knew he was.

He tilted his head in that snake-like way. "Completely. I told you, Poe Dupin, the longer you deny me, the more I'll take from you first." He folded his napkin and set it on the table. "I've invited you here today because you get to choose which one I take as my sacrifice."

The blood drained from my face, and my fists clenched. Before I could hurtle the table, two goons grabbed hold of me. I struggled and called him every name I could think of. He stayed in that same pose, drinking in every ounce of my pain and horror. When I finally stopped struggling, he grinned.

"Tomorrow at noon, I'll come to your area. I'll expect you to hand over your choice."

"Fuck you—"

A blow to the side of my head made everything go dark.

7

I awoke on the sidewalk in front of my shop. I blinked. For a moment, I couldn't remember how I got there, and then everything came rushing back. I gasped and sat up. Dizziness overcame me, and I vomited.

"Poe! Are you okay?" Ollie rushed to my side, with Kennedy right behind.

"What happened?" Kennedy knelt and let me rest my head in her lap.

I took slow breaths. Inhale. Exhale. Until the nausea passed. She helped me sit up, letting me lean heavily against her. Ollie handed me a glass of water. I hadn't even noticed that he'd gone back in the shop for it. My hands shook as I took it. Swishing the water around in my mouth, I spat out a mouthful. Blech. I forced myself to take a few sips and swallow.

I handed the glass back, and with Kennedy's help made it to my feet. I felt unsteady, but that may not have been the concussion so much as the choice Briggs laid at my feet. How could Ethan allow one of his children to be sacrificed?

I was gonna be sick again. I pushed away from Kennedy and leaned against the wall while I lost the rest of my stomach's meager contents. When I finished, Kennedy and Ollie brought me inside and sat me down on a stool.

Before either could ask me again what was wrong, I told them about the terrible choice placed in my hands.

I couldn't do it.

Wouldn't do it.

Jamie and Lucy.

Kennedy gripped my jacket lapels and gave me a small shake.

Fuck, that made my headache worse, and for a second, I thought I'd be sick again.

"Sorry," she said, gentling her hold. "But we lost you there for a second. You have to stop this."

"How? It's legally binding. I'd have to kill him. And most of his top-tier. I don't have that kind of power."

"You know someone who does." Kennedy lifted an eyebrow.

"Who?" Ollie asked. "You know someone who can help?"

Could Tommy? Would he? What kind of price would he demand? Did it matter? I'd give up my life for Lucy and Jamie. I'd give up everything to keep them safe. Briggs knew that, which is why he didn't take me. Tommy . . . he was a businessman. A demon. Powerful. I could ask. Beg, if he wanted.

"Poe, you're scaring me." Ollie stood behind Kennedy's shoulder. "Who do you know that could take on Briggs Bickley?"

I stood, pulled Kennedy into a quick hug. Patted Ollie on the shoulder. "I gotta go. Kens, if I don't come back, I need you to meet the kids after school. Bring them here for the night." I dug in my wallet and pulled out a twenty. "You can order pizza."

"Drama much? I don't need your money. And everything will be *fine*." She looked so sure of it.

Wish I felt the same. Every ask increased the demon's price. I wasn't the sharpest bird in the flock, but I wasn't a complete idiot, either. I might pay it with my life.

Ollie looked between us. "What are you planning—"

"You can't say anything, Ollie. I don't want to freak everyone out more than they already are."

"Okay, but what's going on?"

"Kens can fill you in after I go. Remember," I pointed at him, "you need to keep this a secret."

He hesitated before nodding.

I placed my hand on his shoulder and squeezed, looked him in the eye. I needed him to do this for me.

He didn't flinch. After a moment, he licked his lips, and said, "You got it."

Before I could second-guess myself, I strode out of the store.

~

Tommy probably knew the moment I crossed into his Neighborhood. Wouldn't surprise me, anyway. And what would I tell him? Ethan Short was a waste of feathers and beak. The twins were innocents. But that wasn't Tommy's problem.

I crossed the street and made for Rumpled Still. The shop looked so harmless, but the creature inside was anything but. And yet he was the best chance I had. I took a deep breath. I needed to pull it together. A demon would take advantage if he could. I yanked at my jacket and straightened my shoulders.

The bell tinkled as I swaggered inside and over to the desk to talk to Carter. Tommy noticed me right away in the mirror. I couldn't help but watch him watch me. I shivered.

Magnetic. How I ever thought he was harmless, I couldn't imagine now. He all but sparked with magic. He was cutting the hair of some guy who was talking loudly about his fancy new car. Tommy nodded like he was listening but raised a brow in our direction, so that Carter nodded back.

"Wow, you out partying too late last night, rockstar?" Carter snapped his gum.

"Something like that." My voice sounded wrecked. I turned away from the mirror and faced him.

"Looks like you got run over by the tour bus."

"Thanks." I didn't have the energy to spar with the cat at the moment.

Carter frowned and waved me to the waiting area. "Have a seat before you fall down."

I did as he suggested, and a moment later, he handed me a large bottle of water.

"Looks like you could use some hydration." He didn't even sound snarky when he said it. I must've looked terrible. I needed to pull it together. But I gratefully drank the water down.

After what seemed like forever, Tommy finished with the guy's hair. The rich douche was still going on about the features of his fancy car. The fact that Tommy feigned interest so well was almost scary. Maybe it wasn't an act. Hell, for all I knew, he loved expensive toys.

As soon as his client stepped away, Tommy cleaned up his area and then waved me over.

"Back so soon, sugar?" His voice didn't convey any emotion.

I went to run a hand through my hair in a nervous gesture, but stopped myself. Instead, I straightened my spine, bearding the demon in his den. "I was hoping to make another deal."

"Have a seat, birdie, and tell me all about it." Tommy batted his lashes and draped the cape around me once I'd sat down.

I glowered. "I didn't think you'd want me wasting your time. You seem to have a lot of clients." If my voice came out a little harsh, he didn't seem to notice.

"So what can I do for you, Poe?" He grabbed a pair of scissors.

"I don't need a haircut."

"I'll be the judge of that." Tommy began to run a comb through my hair.

I huffed but allowed him to work. Whatever. It was just hair. I needed to be strategic about how I introduced the topic. Soft pedal? Go straight to the crux? Either way he had the upper hand. His damn apple scent was distracting. Probably meant to put creatures at a disadvantage in their dealings with him.

"You gonna tell me why the caged bird sings?" Tommy almost clipped off a hunk of my hair when I jerked forward and spun to look at him.

"You've heard." I glared.

"About the blood debt? I do keep my ear to the ground. Now, turn back around and stay still, sugar. I could've taken off your ear. Or even worse, messed up your haircut. I've a reputation to maintain." He yanked me back with surprising strength and settled me in the barber chair.

I glared daggers at him in the mirror.

"Ooh, that's kind of hot." Tommy winked at my reflection.

"So, you know what I need."

"I'm not saving Ethan Short's life. I told you, your roost would be better off without him. This is your chance."

Before I could say anything, he added, "I don't usually

give my clients advice, but your heart's in the right place, Poe. If I were you, once I finish, I'd get up, walk out that door, and never darken my doorstep again."

My fists were clenched in my lap. I stayed still but barely. "You don't understand."

"So enlighten me, sugar."

"I don't give a shit about my stepdad's life. He can rot. But Briggs doesn't plan to take the blood debt from Ethan."

Tommy's scissors stilled. "You are *not* a blood relative."

"No, but my half-siblings are." I went on to explain the rest, including Briggs' demand that I choose which child would be sacrificed.

Tommy's expression blanked when I mentioned the kids. For a moment, I could swear his nails became claws, but when I looked again, they were just fingernails. His scissors took up a steady rhythm, and I waited. And waited.

When he finally finished, he removed the cape and shook it.

"You can pay Carter now." He turned around, as though he was going to head to the back.

"So, you won't bargain with me?" I probably said it a little too loud. The whole shop hushed.

Tommy spun back around, his face not-so-neutral now. His eyes glowed that fierce red. He clapped his hands, and some sort of magical bubble appeared around us. He stepped up and caged me in the chair, nose to nose.

"I never said that, sugar. The price just goes up."

"Name your price."

"State specifically what you're bargaining for. Use your words carefully."

"I want to save Jamie and Lucy's lives. I need to protect them."

He sighed. "I can't break the blood debt, but I can save them."

"How?"

"That's for me to know. You only need to worry about what you're willing to give up for this bargain."

"Which is?" I could barely breathe, but what choice did I have?

"I want two things." Tommy straightened up and circled around me, tapping his chin.

"Two? That's not the way it's supposed to work."

"It works however I want it to, birdie."

I huffed. Tommy just grinned, his fangs peeking out.

"What two things?" I finally gritted out. Wasn't like I wouldn't give him whatever he wanted.

Tommy continued to pace, the magic still surrounding us. "First, I need to retrieve something in Josephine Jones' territory. A necklace. I want your help in retrieving it."

I gave him a crooked smile. This game I knew all too well. "You want me to steal it."

Tommy snorted. "No, sugar, I'll pick it up. I want you to accompany me."

"Why me? If you need a bodyguard, you've got one of your wolves who I'm sure would do just as good of a job." I nodded to one of the guards in the mirror.

"I don't need a bodyguard, though that's sweet that you think so." He looked so fucking amused, it was insulting.

"Then what do you need?" I tried not to frown but probably failed miserably.

"Ravens are exceptional lookouts. And of course, thieves. But it's your phone ID I'm interested in utilizing. Briggs hasn't officially annexed your territory yet, right? Josephine still technically owns your strip of Baltimore, so I want to use your ID to enter her Neighborhood. Josephine and I have no troubles, and I'd like to keep it that way. You will act as an extra set of eyes and get us into her Neighborhood without raising any eyebrows. I need this necklace, and my source won't meet me in my Neighborhood. Or even in the neutral zone."

I thought about what he said. "That's sketchy as hell."

Tommy chuckled. "You think? It's bound to be some kind of trap."

"Then why meet him?"

"Her. And everyone eventually gives the devil his due." Tommy stepped up to me and ran his fingers through my hair, massaging the scalp as he went. For just a second, my eyes fluttered closed. He let his claws extend a little from his fingertips and continued the massage.

I stayed silent until Tommy finished. "You sure this item is worth it?"

"Quite sure."

"You said you wanted two things." This next one had to be the knockout punch. I braced for it.

"Hmm, I did, didn't I?" he brushed a lock of hair away from my forehead before taking the cape off. "I want a 51 percent stake in your business."

I slowly stood up. I towered over Tommy, but he wasn't afraid. Part of me wanted to take a swing, but the other part of me wanted to pull Tommy into a hug. Majority share of my shop? He could have taken the whole thing, and I would've gladly given it to him. As much as owning my own business meant to me, it was nothing when compared with my siblings.

"I didn't know you wanted a jewelry store."

"Demons like pretty things. I'm only asking for half. See, I'm a nice fellow." He managed not to laugh as he said it. Demons were many things—mischievous, powerful, sexy—

but no one accused them of being nice. He ran a finger down my chest, then spun and headed to the desk. The magic bubble dissolved. "Carter, take care of Poe, please."

"Wait! You didn't let me respond."

"Your determination is like a bright light in the fog. All I need are the words," he called over his shoulder.

I crossed my arms trying to still a shiver. "Fine. I agree to your terms."

Once again, a clap of thunder sounded in the shop.

Tommy ran his hand along the counter, back and forth. For a moment, he looked almost sad. He nodded. "Then it looks like we have a deal, birdie."

8

I met Tommy back at Rumpled Still later that night. Ollie had agreed to stay with the twins until I returned, and they'd settled in to binge old *Twilight Zone* clips. The barbershop's door was locked when I arrived, though a slender Siamese cat sat on the counter bathing. I knocked. The cat continued to bathe.

I knocked again. The cat looked up, then placed his other leg high in the air and went back to his bath.

When Tommy came to the front of the shop, he paused when he saw me at the door. He wore black skinny jeans, a gray oversized hoodie, and a pair of Chucks. What was he, twelve? And yet I had the urge to strip off the sweatshirt to see what was underneath. It would be a lot more comfortable if Tommy wasn't quite so delectable.

Fuck demons and their wiles. Had to be an incubus. Only explanation why I sported wood every time he came near me. Felt like a teenager.

Tommy smiled as if he could read my thoughts. For all I knew, he could. His smile melted away as he glowered at the cat and said something.

The cat hopped off the counter and transformed back into Carter Strike. Fuck. I should've known. Stupid cat shifter. He wore a skintight silver shirt and leather pants that looked painted on. Heeled, bright pink boots topped off his outfit. Clubbing gear. He sauntered over to the door and unlocked it. He smiled at me like he'd just drunk a delicious bowl of cream.

He held the door open for Tommy, then locked up behind his boss after they exited.

"Good luck, rockstar. You'll need it." Carter nudged me with his hip as he strolled past. "See ya tomorrow, Boss."

Tommy's lips turned up in the hint of a smile. He watched Carter until the cat disappeared around a corner, before turning back to me. He didn't look like he was dressed for the occasion.

I wore all black and added a balaclava around my neck. Never knew when it would come in handy. I also wore a pair of butter-soft black gloves, one of many pairs I owned.

"My, my, don't you look like you're ready to steal the president's tiara." He gave me a thorough once-over, his expression more considering than salacious.

"Better to be prepared."

"Indeed."

"It would have been better if you'd told me exactly where we're going. I could have checked it out. I don't normally go someplace without knowing what I'll encounter. Or if there are escape routes. You sure you want to do this?"

"Quite sure." He nodded.

"It's your hide."

A moment later, a sleek black limo pulled up beside us. I recognized one of the wolf shifters from the shop. I quirked a brow. "So much for incognito."

"If it's a trap, I'd at least like to show up in style." Tommy didn't laugh, but his voice sounded amused.

What the hell had I signed up for? Clearly he didn't

really need my ID. So, why was I there? Before I could ask, a wolf shifter hopped out and held the door open for us.

"Thank you, Michael." Tommy slid into the backseat, and I followed.

After we were underway, Tommy pushed a button. The window slid up between us and the driver.

"That's better. Now we can speak freely." Tommy ran a hand through his hair, and I could swear it now glittered.

I had a bunch of questions, but instead I sank down into the well-cushioned leather seats and waited.

"Ooh, very good. I like a man who knows when to be quiet."

I snorted. I rarely kept my mouth shut. He didn't need to know that.

"Layla Lupine is one of Josephine's personal guards. She's had access to this particular item for a number of weeks. I haven't had time in my schedule to pick it up until now. It's supposed to be an easy exchange."

"Uh-huh."

"Exactly." Tommy kept quiet and looked out the window. He ran a finger absently over one of his hoodie's cuffs.

"If you know it's a trap, why are we doing this?" I finally asked.

"I don't know that it's a trap, birdie, I just suspect it. It *could* be an easy exchange."

"You don't believe that."

"No. Then again, I've had more than two-thousand years to study this world. Nothing surprises me anymore."

Two-thousand years? Crow and raven shifters could live close to two-hundred years. What would it be like to be more than two-*thousand* years old?

"Why do you want to walk into a trap?"

"Why not?"

"Are you so confident you'll come out of it in one piece?"

"Oh, yes. My pieces aren't the ones you need to worry about." Tommy's eyes glinted red in the dim light of the car.

"Then why am I here? You said you don't need me to steal it. And you clearly don't need my ID."

"No." Tommy reached over and gripped my knee, before releasing me. "But you want my help, so I demand yours in return."

"How can I help? My only skills are as a thief." I ran my hands over my thighs. What was I getting myself into?

"Not true. But don't worry about it, sugar. You won't be in any danger."

Huh. Not exactly an answer, but I could tell he wasn't giving me any more. As much as it pissed me off, what did it matter? He could pretty much ask me to walk into hell to steal Satan's pitchfork. I'd do it if it meant keeping the twins safe.

"You don't think she'll show up with it," I said.

"She'll show up with it. I'd know if she didn't right away. But that doesn't mean she won't try to trick me."

"How would you know what she plans?"

Tommy chewed on his bottom lip and seemed to consider this.

How could such an innocent move send a rush of heat through my gut?

Tommy gave me a knowing leer. "Later, sugar."

I forced myself to look away. "You didn't answer my question."

"I'm a demon. We only deal in partial answers."

"Then I'll take a partial answer."

Tommy chuckled. "I like you, Poe. And not just because you fill out those jeans nicely."

"Still not answering," I sing-songed.

Tommy tapped his chin thoughtfully. "I can read anyone's desire. You can't ever lie to me about what you want. If the desire is to hide things from me—like a jewel, for example—all I have to do is glance at you and I know."

I whistled. "That's some power."

"Not all power has to be flash-bang. Sometimes it's the subtle things that are the most potent."

The limo turned onto North Haven and made its way to Highlandtown. Why meet in this area? Ethan called it the hillbilly ghetto because when he was a young raven, Appalachian migrants had settled this area. Not that you'd know it today. A favorite of working-class vampires, Highlandtown seemed like the worst place to have a secret meeting with one of Josephine's minions. The vampires would all be bonded to Josephine. Was Layla another vampire, then?

"You think Josephine's involved in this?" We'd be putting ourselves in vampire central. Perfect place to spring a trap. Could Tommy take on a couple dozen vampires? Just what were the limits of his powers?

"We'll see. But I know Layla didn't get the item from Josephine. She would've had to snag it from either the Hons or more likely the Coven. I asked Layla to look out for it. And promised her heart's desire if she obtained it." The grin he gave me was downright evil and caused a shiver to race down my spine. No twink should be that scary. Just saying.

"You gonna tell me what she desires?"

"Josephine's notice. She wants to move up the ranks."

"Why do I feel like there is a bigger game going on here?"

"Because, my dear Poe, there's always more going on than meets the eye."

I grunted. The demon was frustrating. Though I was

surprised to learn as much as I had. So he'd help her move up in the ranks in order to get this necklace? Lots of creatures did weird things for sparkly items. I was a prime example.

We turned onto Bank Street and pulled up in front of a three-story abandoned building that had at one time been a department store. The row of streetlights were all dark. How convenient. The bottom of the building might have originally been gray, but colorful graffiti made it hard to tell. A large, corrugated vinyl strip that resembled flashing separated the first and second floor and ran the length of the building. Red brick with glass-block windows made up the two top floors. Plywood covered the double doors and surrounding windows.

Nah, this didn't look suspicious. I huffed. Tommy's lips turned up. Yeah, glad *someone* was amused.

"We're just gonna walk into the trap, are we?"

He raised a single brow. "I am. You're going to meet me up there." He pointed to a broken-section of window on the third floor.

"How will I tell you if I see something?"

"Do you think I can't understand the vocalizations of a raven shifter?"

"Of course you can." Why didn't that surprise me at all?

"There are some advantages to my advanced age." With that, Tommy slid out of the limo and left the door cracked so I could transform. I shifted and hopped out of the car.

After a brief pause, I clacked my beak once and launched myself toward the broken glass blocks. Before entering, I took a quick circuit of the building. Since it was connected to another building on one side, I cut up over the roof. Nothing stood out. I flew back toward the window and perched.

Tommy hadn't yet entered. He tapped the top of the limo and stepped to the sidewalk. The car pulled away from the curb and disappeared down the street. He didn't look in my direction, but I could sense he knew exactly where I perched.

He pulled the door open without any resistance. Uh, yeah. Trap. He took a lot more risks than I did.

I turned toward the interior of the building. Dark, though I could see some other birds nesting.

I scanned an area that had once been an open floor plan —probably a display space—with thin brick columns instead of loadbearing walls. I didn't detect anything out of the ordinary. Cracked plaster on the outer walls, a drop ceiling with most of the tiles missing, and exposed pipes. Commonplace. A large skylight over a defunct escalator in the center of the room may have been the building's most notable feature.

I flapped over to the other birds. They cheeped in alarm when they saw me coming.

"Settle," a crow squawked at them before making room for me to perch next to him. "Greetings, large friend. My name is Boldtalon. Why have you invaded our roosts?"

"Apologies, Boldtalon. I am Poe. I do not mean to intrude. I am helping a creature who suspects treachery. I would appreciate it if I am able to remain and assess from this perch." Most raven shifters didn't bother speaking to birds, even ravens. But I'd learned long ago that birds could go almost anywhere in the city, and they made wonderful lookouts and informants. They were also very formal creatures.

"You are granted such, friend. It is not often we watch the follies of no-winged creatures. Should we expect fast metal?" Crows couldn't actually smile, but Boldtalon did the equivalent.

Fast metal? Oh, bullets. "I cannot say for sure, Boldtalon. I would not discount it. And possibly magic as well. My creature is a demon. The other, I think, is a vampire."

"You involve yourself in dangerous issues, Poe."

Tell me about it. "I must protect my nest. A bird does what he can for his chicks."

Boldtalon nodded like this was obvious.

"Only a single no-wing came through today. She came just after dark and resides there." He nodded toward an area against one wall that looked like a pile of ceiling tiles.

I scanned the area. Vampires were exceptional at blending into the dark, but in this form, my eyesight was much sharper than when I was in my no-winged one. Still, I would have missed her if Boldtalon hadn't told me her whereabouts.

"She placed a shiny in each corner. I collected one of them." Boldtalon indicated his nest. A quarter sparkled. Without light, that shouldn't happen.

Interesting. What did it mean?

Talk about a fool's errand. For Tommy. And certainly for me. "It is not a regular shiny."

Boldtalon clacked his beak. "I agree. It glows without light."

"I do not think it safe. These creatures are treacherous."

His head turned. Crows were hoarders by nature. He'd be suspicious of my motives. But I couldn't in good conscience not warn him. He side-eyed the other birds, then his gaze returned to me.

"I shall place it elsewhere. But it is my treasure. Unless others will fight for it."

"I acknowledge your ownership and do not wish to fight."

Boldtalon plucked the quarter from the nest and flew across the expanse to another corner ledge. He dropped it there, then flew back. "Look!" he pointed his beak toward the escalator.

Tommy stepped up the final step. He looked so young and small as he crossed the floor, his hands stuffed into his hoodie's pockets. He walked directly toward the place where the vampire hid.

A female vampire appeared from the dark and waved to Tommy. She smiled, but from my position, I could see that she scanned the area. Maybe she was expecting traps as well.

Tommy stopped and waited for her to approach. His posture spoke of his relaxation. Was he really not afraid or just good at faking it? I didn't have a ton of experience around vampires, but she seemed stiff.

She said a few words that I couldn't hear before Tommy nodded. She then pulled out a thin chain holding a stone smaller than my pinky nail. That was a lot of risks for a small bobble, but with my trained eye, I could see it was much more than a gem.

She handed it over, and Tommy's voice carried. "Good doing business with you, Layla. You sure you're settled on what you want?"

"Of course."

"Then you shall have it."

Several vampires stepped from the escalator. Layla's eyes widened before she lobbed something at Tommy.

No!

9

Tommy waved his hand, and the object burned up. A shimmer rippled the air behind him, and four mages appeared—three in the corners, except to where Boldtalon had taken the quarter. That mage materialized on the much-too-small ledge and shrieked as he fell straight onto a jagged piece of wood that acted like a spear. That had to hurt.

"Look out!" I squawked.

Tommy threw a burst of energy at Layla as she retreated. She screamed as she went down. He spun, but one mage had already released his spell. Another threw a fireball at the oncoming vampires.

The spell struck Tommy and wrapped him in what morphed into a pentagram.

Fuck! Not good. Pentagram spells were not run-of-the-mill. In fact, I could only name two mages in Baltimore who were capable of one. Tommy attempted to escape the pentagram, but it held him tight. He didn't look scared so much as furious, his claws and teeth growing longer and sharper. He roared, his face turning inhuman, and it sent a shiver through my body.

Also arousal, but I was a little fucked up.

Before I could think better of it, I screeched, "We attack!"

I dove from my perch, straight for the mage who'd trapped Tommy. The guy didn't know what hit him. Surprisingly, the other birds swarmed after me and attacked.

We knocked him over, and I swooped toward the pentagram. A bolt of lightning shot past me, followed by a mage's scream. The other birds continued their attack. The vampires had surrounded another magic user. I winged across the pentagram's border and severed the magic. Tommy sprung forward and deflected another bolt of lightning that would have turned me to a ball of charred feathers.

Before the pentagram mage could retreat, Tommy was on him. I dove back into the fray, raking my claws over another mage's arm. She screamed and disappeared in a puff of smoke. My fellow birds cawed in triumph and swooped toward the rafters. I turned back toward Tommy. His claws were embedded in the chest of the magic user. The guy convulsed and foamed at the mouth from the torrent of magic Tommy poured into him. Finally, the mage lay still, a blackened, ruined mess.

The other two mages lay on the ground, dead or unconscious. I couldn't tell. And honestly, didn't care. A woman I recognized as Josephine Jones stood with bloody fangs extended over a cowering Layla. Enforcers ringed Layla while other vampires stood over the mages. When had they all arrived?

Tommy pulled his claws from the dead mage. I fluttered down beside him. Holy fuck! He had just taken out Obrum Drach. Drach was one of the most powerful magic wielders in the U.S. and had dispatched him like he was a gentle lamb gone to slaughter.

Tommy's hands returned to human form. He wiped

them off on Drach's shirt. Not like Drach would need it. Red magic poured out of the deceased mage and into Tommy, just like it had from the man who hadn't fulfilled his bargain.

We made eye contact. Tommy's eyes glowed bright red. For a moment, I feared he didn't recognize me. Then he winked.

Boldtalon landed beside me. Tommy gave the crow a lopsided grin as he knelt by the small pillar of salt that had once been Drach. "Thank you for your service, noble crow. I shall reward you and your brethren well. You are all welcome in my Neighborhood, where I will give you nests lined with the softest materials and place birdfeeders near your roosts that shall always remain full."

While his thanks was impressive enough, the fact he did it in the language of a raven was even more impressive. His accent was posh. Of course it was.

"You are too generous, friend demon. We accept your offer." Boldtalon clacked his beak three times, sealing the deal.

Tommy stood. He held out his arm and nodded for me to rest upon it. Why didn't he want me to change back? I wasn't a falcon, and it was a little weird to hop onto his arm. I puffed up a little. I could so pull off a falcon.

Tommy approached one of the unconscious mages. He held out a hand, and they turned to salt, their essence adding to his magic. He did the same to the other before approaching Josephine.

Josephine Jones was a tall, powerfully built woman. Her dark skin made her fangs stand out, and her golden eyes assessed us as we approached. Fierce and unafraid.

She tilted her chin slightly, her fangs slowly retracting.

"Seems you were right, Tommy. I didn't suspect Susannah of such treachery."

Wait. Susannah Moore? The Roger of West Baltimore? She was somehow involved in this mess? I tilted my head in question but Tommy ignored me.

"Unfortunately, Jos. I had hoped this wasn't the play. But it makes sense." Tommy absently stroked my back feathers.

She nodded. "I will talk to Angel and Bengal. The other Rogers will want to know."

Layla Lupine looked up at Tommy from where she lay on the ground. One of the large enforcers had a foot on her back, keeping her in place. "You broke our deal, demon," she rasped out.

"Did I?" Tommy smirked. "I gave you what you asked for."

"I asked for Josephine to promote me above all others. Not kill me."

Tommy's grin grew larger. He snapped his fingers and a contract appeared. He unrolled it. "No, you specifically asked for her to *notice you*. And now she has. If you wanted to be her right-hand, you never would have tried to bring Susannah's people into this Neighborhood without Josephine's knowledge. You wanted your cake and to eat it, too. Jos values loyalty, not shortcuts."

Layla was hauled up by a particularly fierce-looking enforcer. His eyes glowed almost as red as Tommy's when he looked at her. They weren't gonna go easy on her.

Not my problem. Or Tommy's.

"Nice doing business with you, Jos." Tommy nodded.

"Indeed." She turned and disappeared down the escalator. Within moments, the vampires were all gone.

"We should get out of here, Poe." Tommy spun around

as two more mages appeared. "Seems Susannah's not pleased that Obrum didn't return."

As the Roger for West Baltimore, Susannah Moore's coven was one of the most powerful in the country. Obrum Drach had been her consort. Past tense.

A fireball came straight toward us. Tommy deflected the magic like it was a gnat, with a simple flick of the wrist. I couldn't be quite so relaxed. I hopped onto his shoulder, grabbed his hoodie, and launched myself into the air.

Tommy laughed when we went airborne. I might not be much bigger than the average raven, but I was a lot stronger. Carrying him wasn't too much of a burden. Tommy threw something at the mages as we sailed out of one of the broken windows. A moment later, two clouds of red magic merged with his own. Damn, he was good.

I flew toward where I figured the limo would be waiting. Tommy pointed to the right, and I corrected course. When I saw the car, I descended and landed next to it. Releasing my grip on Tommy's hoodie, I hopped to the ground and shifted to my human form, my clothes also reappearing with the transformation. Tommy pulled open the door and jumped into the back of the car. He snagged my hand and tugged me in behind.

"Hit it, Michael," he said through the intercom.

The limo shot forward and skidded around a corner, throwing me into Tommy. Tommy laughed and clasped my hair, pulling me into a liquid-fire kiss. I barely had time to react before Tommy climbed on my lap and ran his tongue against my lips, asking for entrance.

Maybe it was the adrenaline, or the fact that Tommy was just that hot, but I opened for him. Tommy took advantage and slid his tongue against mine in a mind-melting caress.

He tasted of warm apples. My arms went around him and pulled him close as we ate at each other.

We broke apart. Tommy's eyes were luminescent violet, and his lips kiss-swollen, with his fangs peeking out.

"Ever had sex in a limo, birdie?"

10

"No." I swallowed. "Never in a limo."

"I like being your first." Tommy ran a finger across my jaw. His finger was now tipped with a claw. I shuddered but didn't pull away. Something about him being such a dangerous creature made my dick leap against my zipper.

Tommy grabbed my wrist and peeled off my glove, and then did the same with the other. He then tossed them aside, and popped the button on my jeans and slowly lowered the zipper. He reached a small hand inside my boxer briefs and pulled out my very stiff cock.

"Mmm, nice. Very nice." Tommy stroked me a few times and reconnected our mouths.

Never one to be a slacker, I reached between us and tugged at Tommy's hoodie. He released me long enough for me to pull it over his head and drop it on the seat beside us. His shirt went next. With only a few curses, Tommy wiggled out of his jeans and Chucks, only leaving his socks. They were rainbow-colored. Of course.

Tommy reached into a pocket on the car door and pulled out lube. He didn't bother with condoms. Shifters couldn't pass disease, and demons probably couldn't, either. Tommy then snapped open the lid of the lube and trickled some onto my cock. I hissed from the coolness, Tommy's hand closed around me and stroked several times, which warmed things up quite nicely. He then clambered back onto my lap and lined himself up.

"You're gonna hurt yourself."

"I like a bit of pain," Tommy said, sliding onto my cock. He didn't go slow, slamming against my pelvis. "Fuck, you're big."

I groaned and clasped his hips. I tried my best to give him time to adjust. Bit my lip to pull my thoughts away from where we were connected.

You think a two-thousand-year-old demon would be pretty well broken in, but you'd be wrong. Tommy's compact body was so tight it was almost painful. But in the best way possible.

"Damn, you feel good." Hell yeah, he did.

Tommy draped his arm around my shoulders. "You ain't felt nothing yet, sugar."

I believed it. He set up a sensual rhythm, neither too fast nor too slow. His body gliding down to meet each of my thrusts. I growled, my fingers probably leaving bruises on his hips. Tommy didn't seem to mind. If anything, it spurred him on.

I wanted to believe that I was just slaking my lust with his body, but damn, the demon felt so right. I suppose all incubi did. When I'd seen Obrum Drach trap Tommy, I'd reacted automatically. The idea that someone would cage him enraged me. If I had more brain cells at my disposal, I might wonder why that was the case. With each glide, each slide of Tommy's body, I succumbed to his charms. I swore, and Tommy laughed.

"So responsive," Tommy said, running his tongue over my jaw.

"Such a bossy bottom," I retorted.

"Guilty. But to be fair . . ." Tommy panted as I slammed him down on my cock. "I'm also a bossy top."

I groaned. I believed it. I thrust, my body's needs taking over. I lost myself in the heat and the ecstasy. "I am gonna make you feel it for a week," I snarled.

"You'd better." Tommy tore my balaclava from my neck and pulled the neckline of my shirt down so he could suck up marks all along my collarbone.

Normally I didn't like it when guys marked me. It smacked too much of ownership, and I was a free bird. But Tommy's marks and the suction made my head spin and my dick grow harder. Something hot about wearing his brand. Not that I'd ever fucking tell him.

He bounced on my lap, and I could feel my balls pull up tight. I was getting close. I gripped his hips and angled him a bit. When he gasped and his claw-tipped fingers dug into my shoulders—damn that was hot—I knew I was on the right track. I pegged his prostate again and again, and he writhed on my lap.

He let go with one hand and wrapped it around his dick. He stroked in time to our rhythm, puffs and pants spilling from his mouth. His eyes widened, then turned red, and his body tightened around me like a vice. He pulled my shirt up, gripping it in his fist. I slammed our mouths together as he climaxed and swallowed his grunts.

So close, I sped up as I went over the edge, too. The pleasure blinded me for a moment.

When I came back to Earth, Tommy was collapsed on my chest, giggling. I'd never heard him make that sound before. Adorable. Which was weird when I'd just seen him kill one of the most powerful magic users of our day. Meh, I'd go with it.

I placed a kiss on the top of his head before I realized

what I was doing. Fuck it. I could claim it was residual afterglow.

Tommy didn't pull away. Instead, he snuggled in, rested his head on my shoulder. "I love a good adventure."

I laughed. Couldn't help myself. "You know who you killed, right?"

Tommy shrugged. "Drach had it coming. All that posturing. He's always been insufferable. Susannah not much better."

"Can I ask you something?"

"Sure, sugar. Can't promise I'll answer, though."

"That red haze that you absorb when you kill someone? Is that their life force? Or their soul? Or their magic?"

Tommy leaned back for a second and placed a gentle kiss on my lips. "Something like that."

"And you feed off of it? Or it becomes yours?"

"Mmhmm."

Okay, this wasn't getting me anywhere. Did I mention that demons were frustrating?

We lay there for a bit until the limo crossed back into raven territory. Tommy slid off my lap and began to dress. My stomach and pelvis were sticky as hell, and the come was beginning to dry. And itch. I'd have to shower when I got home.

The limo turned onto my street. How did he know where I lived? Not that it was a big secret or anything. Tommy had already pulled on his jeans and hoodie and used his T-shirt to help clean me up. I just had time to tuck myself back in, zip up, and get my shirt pulled down when the limo stopped in front of my shop.

"Thank you, sugar. You made for a wild ride." Tommy leaned in and pressed his lips gently to mine. When he leaned back, his eyes were soft. Within seconds, they hardened. "You need to get rid of your alpha. If you don't, you'll be darkening my doorstep again. Each time you ask, the price gets higher."

If that wasn't a frigid jug of water tossed in my face, I didn't know what was. "Don't worry, this should take care of things. I won't be back for any favors."

Tommy leaned into me again, looking debauched, and so sexy that my cock twitched. Yet Tommy had been pretty clear. There was always a price. We locked gazes. As I slid toward the door. Tommy held up a hand. "You'll be back, birdie. They always come back."

Before we could start our awkward goodbyes, Tommy pushed the door open and climbed out. What the hell?

The twins stood on the stoop with Ollie and Kennedy. What was she doing here? Ollie gave me a sheepish smile; she grinned full wattage. The kids rushed me and threw their arms around my waist.

"We were worried," Lucy scolded. "Ollie said you'd be out all night. We were going to come find you."

Ollie shook his head subtly to let me know they hadn't actually planned to do that. Though Lucy would if given half a chance.

"What are you guys doing up? It's way past your bedtime."

"Ollie is bad at enforcing rules." Lucy grinned.

Ollie blushed to the roots of his hair.

"Tommy!" Kennedy stepped forward, and they exchanged air kisses. "It's been too long."

Tommy grinned, his fangs peeking out. "Saw your ex-fiancé the other day. He's still an asshole."

Kennedy growled. "We were engaged for like five seconds, and you'll never let me live it down."

Tommy shrugged. "What can I say? Demons have long memories."

"Speaking of long memories—"

"Little ears, my dear. Let's not reminisce quite yet."

"Fine. But you owe me."

"Do I?"

They stared each other down. Uh, what?

"You know you do." She gave him a cat-that-swallowed-the-canary grin.

"Maybe." He didn't look amused.

She smirked, "Definitely. We can discuss that later." She side-eyed me.

"You two know each other?" I asked. Tommy just smirked and knelt down to say hello to the twins, leaving Kennedy to me.

"Obviously, hon. You think I would've sent you to a demon without having vetted him first? What kind of friend do you think I am?" She huffed.

"You could've told me. I went there all freaked out. And it turns out you guys are old buddies. Geez, Kens. Warn a guy next time." What the hell?

"You did fine. Besides, if I'd warned you, you would've acted weird."

"I think the word you're looking for is 'comfortable'. It wasn't easy showing up and asking him for a favor. If I'd known you were friends, I wouldn't have felt quite as strange about it."

"Yes, you would've, hon. You hate asking anyone for anything. It was better this way. Trust me."

"Said the fox to the hens."

Kennedy stepped close and hugged me. She whispered in my ear, "You can trust him. He won't steer you wrong. But make sure you shower, 'kay? You reek of sex."

I pulled away, glared. She continued grinning, pretended to straighten an invisible halo.

Yeah, right.

Tommy was still crouched down, and he and the twins were having quite an animated, but whispered conversation. Lucy smacked her hand over her mouth and giggled. Jamie's eyes were huge, and he shook his head.

Kennedy leaned in to me and said, "See, he's good with kids, too."

I narrowed my eyes. Was she . . . matchmaking? Or did she mean he was trustworthy? Her innocent demeanor didn't fool me anymore when it came to business, but she'd never encouraged me to date someone before. Or was I reading this wrong?

Tommy stood and turned toward us. "A pleasure as always, Kennedy. You need to come round, so we can go for drinks one night and catch up. It seems your life has taken an interesting turn."

She grinned. "You could say that. Mind if I catch a ride with you?"

He raised a brow, nodded toward the limo.

"Cool." She leaned in and kissed my cheek. "Later, Poe. Remember what I said."

Kennedy waved to Michael as she approached the limo. He dashed out and held the door for her.

Tommy stepped into my space and placed his hand in the crook of my arm. "Walk me back to my car, sugar."

He wasn't asking.

"Ollie, take them back inside, would ya? The kids are up way past their bedtime." I gave them both a stern look.

Jamie ducked his head, but Lucy stuck her tongue out.

Tommy said good night to Ollie and the kids. He steered me slowly toward the limo.

"Listen carefully, Poe. Tomorrow, when Briggs shows up, he's going to ask you to pick one of the children. You need to pick Lucy. She's—"

"No! What the fuck? You said you could save them! You said—"

"Poe, hush." He kept his voice low, but it was like a hand closed around my throat.

I struggled against the feeling for a second, then gave in.

"That's better," he said. "Now, you need to pick Lucy. She's the braver of the two. Once you choose her, you must trust that things will be okay. And when everything is done, you *must* ask Briggs whether the blood debt is settled. This is very important, sugar. Do as I say, and you will get your heart's desire. Fail to follow my advice, and there will be a tragic outcome."

"But—"

"Goodnight, Poe Dupin." He went up on tiptoes and placed a kiss on my lips before ducking back into the limo.

The door slammed, and the car sped away.

11

I rose early after a sleepless night and made French toast. I moved around the kitchenette quietly, not wanting to wake the kids. I didn't have a lot. A small dorm-sized fridge, a hotplate, some old pans and two banged up skillets. I owned a small microwave, toaster oven, and crock pot, but not enough counter space to keep them in the open. Sawhorses with a plywood top acted as my counter, and I used a rickety card table to eat on since I didn't have room for anything larger.

I added a dash more vanilla to the batter. When the twins got up, we ate.

Jamie and I were jittery, picking at our food, but Lucy ate like a champ, seemingly unconcerned. She'd braided her hair herself, and wore a flowery purple shirt with a pair of bedazzled jeans. Jamie dressed more casually in athletic pants and a tee. Both looked so innocent. Were innocent. How could their dad do this to them?

And how could I explain this to them? It was too much to ask of any nine-year-old.

I could take them and run. Stupid idea. We'd never get far. Especially since the twins weren't old enough to shift yet. That wouldn't happen until sometime around their sixteenth birthday.

After Lucy shoved in the last bite, she grinned at me

with syrup around her mouth and patted her shirt above her heart. "Don't worry, Poe. Everything will be okay."

Ah, to have the confidence of a kid again.

"You don't even know what I'm gonna ask of you, Luce."

"I know you're supposed to choose me. I'm good with it."

My jaw clenched. What had Tommy said to her? Good with it? What did she think would happen? Before I could decide how much to tell her, car horns honking cut off my explanation. They shouldn't be here yet. Damn Briggs!

Jamie covered his ears, never one for lots of noise. But Lucy remained calm. Too calm.

I didn't have time to figure out what was going on. The honking had grown louder and more persistent. I could hear our neighbors shouting and their dogs barking. Lucy jumped up from the table and grabbed my hand and tugged me to my feet.

"It's okay," she repeated.

But it wasn't. I gripped her hand tightly, her small fingers interlaced with mine.

"Jamie, I need you to stay here." No reason he had to see this.

Jamie, who looked so much like my mom, tipped his chin at that same angle my mom had used to steel herself for something unpleasant. He took his hands off his ears and reached for my other hand.

"I'm coming," he said, standing.

"No, you—"

"Your friend said you'd need me." Jamie didn't dig in his heels often—that was Lucy's role—but when he did, he didn't budge. And how much *had* Tommy said to them last night? Why would I need him there? I rubbed at my forehead.

Another horn blast.

I clasped both kids to me. My knees shook, and it would be a miracle if I didn't throw up. I wish I had the power to wipe Briggs Bickley and his ilk from Charm City. I lowered myself to their level and made eye contact with both in turn.

"Luce, I need you to be very brave and to trust me." My stomach soured saying it. How would Tommy prevent her from being turned to stone? What if...

No! I had to believe.

"I do trust you." She nodded. "Just make sure Jamie doesn't freak out."

"I don't freak out—" he said, his face turning red.

Another, longer horn blast cut off his indignation. Fuck. Out of time. I straightened and kept ahold of both their hands. We walked through the front of the shop and peered out the front door.

Briggs had arrived in his snakeskin Hummer. Several other SUVs, all with his snakehead logo, had pulled alongside, blocking the road.

His entourage disembarked and spread out, probably checking for traps. Andre eventually nodded, and Briggs stepped out of the back of the Hummer.

A moment later another door opened, and my stepdad emerged from the other side. Fucker. He wore a suit that couldn't be his, and he stumbled a bit. Drunk. He didn't meet any of our eyes, instead focusing on Briggs.

We stepped from the shop.

By now, most of our roost had gathered around on the sidewalk. They muttered among themselves, the tang of fear sharp in the air.

Briggs stepped forward, and a hush fell over the crowd. He unrolled the same parchment I'd seen the day before. "I'm owed a blood debt. Ethan Short killed a member of my

Neighborhood. Because I recognize the importance of your alpha to the roost, I have spared his life."

A collective sigh went up among the roost.

"However, the blood debt remains. I have tasked Poe Dupin to choose which of the Short children will take their father's place. Have you made that decision, Poe?"

He grinned. It was so evil that I'm surprised the pavement didn't melt. The roost raised angry voices in protest. Andre and Briggs' other enforcers stepped forward carrying heavy firepower. Probably silver bullets in the guns. Shifters couldn't heal with silver in them and it caused them to shift back to their humanoid form.

Bastards.

I couldn't do it. My hands tightened around both of the twins. I willed my tongue to work, but I couldn't find the words to condemn Lucy. It was one thing for Tommy to say, "Trust me," but another for me to actually do it. Tommy always kept his bargains. Always. Still, my voice wouldn't come.

Lucy's and my hand shot into the air. She'd chosen for me. I sucked in a breath and let it out slowly.

"While I find your terms to be despicable, Ethan Short, the roost's alpha made a binding deal with you, sealing the fate of one of his offspring." I glared at Ethan, all but ignoring Briggs. Not only would that piss off Briggs, but I wanted everyone in the roost to know what he had done. He, of course, didn't meet my condemning gaze. That was fine. For now.

"Since I must choose, I've selected . . . Lucy." Saying the words was like a knife to the heart. Faith. Belief. Trust. Things I lacked.

Ethan didn't even flinch. Nor did he look our way. Did he even care?

I went to step forward with Lucy, but she shook her fingers out of my hand. She threw herself into my arms and then pulled away and hugged Jamie. My lip trembled, but I couldn't still it. She walked toward Briggs, not showing any fear, her pigtails making her look oddly defiant.

I took a step to grab her and pull her back, but Jamie grasped my hand. "You have to have faith," he said. "Your friend said so."

Andre signaled to two large enforcers who then stepped into my path. Nothing like a little insurance on their part. Rage burned bright. *Please, Tommy, don't disappoint*. Not a lot of good in this world, but these two kids—they made everything worth it.

I swallowed and held my ground. The hardest thing I've ever done. If I could kill Briggs, I wouldn't hesitate.

Briggs seemed surprised that I'd chosen and more surprised that Lucy wasn't cowering or crying. Not my Lucy.

She stood with her chin tilted at a rebellious angle and her arms crossed. Briggs approached her, and his eyes shifted to an unnatural yellow, his pupil slitted like a snake's. She stood her ground.

He lunged, and she yelped and leaned back. That's when the bastard struck. He shot light from his eyes like a laser.

It struck her full on in the face.

She gasped, and then with a crackling sound, she turned to stone.

The crowd gasped and some cried out.

I screamed. Tommy had betrayed me! I tried to rush around Briggs' enforcers to get to Lucy. It had to be a mistake!

They moved into my path, blocking me.

"You fucking bastard!" I shouted at Briggs. I wanted to kill him, I wanted—

"Poe," Jamie's trembling voice broke through my rage and pain. "Remember to *ask*."

Ask? Tommy said I had to ask about the blood debt. But he hadn't kept his word. Had he? I forced myself to grit out, "Is the blood debt settled?"

Briggs chuckled, like we were talking about the fucking weather and not my little sister's life. He stuffed his hands in his pants pockets, a smug grin on his reptilian face.

"It's settled." He snapped his fingers, and his enforcers moved out of my way.

I'd never hated anyone like I hated him at that moment. Jamie held my hand in a death-grip as we approached Lucy.

Her statue shimmered, and the same crackling sounded again. Green light engulfed her. One moment she was a statue. The next, a girl.

I gasped and wasn't the only one. Briggs gaped, his forked tongue evident.

"See, Poe. I'm okay. Just like your friend said I would be." Lucy reached up and pulled down the collar of her shirt. She wore the necklace Tommy collected last night.

So many questions, but they could wait. I pulled her into my arms and yanked Jamie in, too.

"What's the meaning of this?" Briggs' voice resonated with fury.

I released the twins, placing them behind me. "We gave you your blood debt, now we're even."

"She lives."

"You turned her to stone. You voided the blood debt."

Briggs' enforcers moved to box us in. The twins could never outrun them. A few roost members crowded in close, prepared to fight, including Abe. Others stepped back.

There were too many of Briggs' people. And not enough of us.

A familiar limo cruised down the opposite end of our street from where Briggs and his entourage had blocked the road. The limo came to a stop in front of Spun Gold Jewelers. Michael jumped out from the driver's side and hurried to open the back door.

Tommy Tittoti stepped out in a black bespoke suit that fit his trim build in a way that made me jealous of the material. I wanted to wrap around him just like that.

If the tension affected Tommy, you'd never know it. He moved with inhuman grace, past the first line of enforcers. One made a move to grab him and, within the blink of an eye, turned into a pile of salt. The creature's life force zipped into Tommy as his magic absorbed it.

He didn't even pause. Stepped next to me. Faced Briggs.

"Briggs, I believe you've concluded your business here." His eyes glowed that eerie red, and he looked larger, his magic crackling around him. And holy shit! His shadow! It had wings and a barbed tail. Horns, cloven hooves, and a long snout. I blinked and it was gone.

Even from the distance, I could see the muscle in Briggs' jaw twitch. "I was just speaking to my friend, Poe."

"No, you were speaking to *my* friend, Poe."

Briggs stiffened. "So that's how it is?"

Tommy inclined his head.

Briggs and Tommy continued to stare each other down. Briggs whistled. I braced for the fight. But his enforcers withdrew.

Briggs turned to go, but called over his shoulder, "Pity, Poe. We would've had so much fun together."

I snorted but managed not to tell him to fuck right off. Tommy didn't move until Briggs and his contingent had loaded into their cars and driven away.

Once it was just the roost and Tommy, his eyes dimmed

to their gorgeous purple, and he held out a fist to Lucy, who gave him a fist bump.

"Told you it would work," Tommy said.

"It was so cool! I'm gonna flex and tell everyone at school a basilisk turned me to stone. Janelle will be sooo jelly." Lucy beamed, like it hadn't been the scariest moment of my entire life. She handed back the necklace, and he pocketed it.

I rubbed my hands over my face, the adrenaline of moments ago making me feel a little shaky. Tommy placed a hand on my back and rubbed little circles. "It's okay, sugar. She's okay."

"You could've told me," I said between my fingers. God, when I'd thought . . .

"I could have. But—no offense—you would've tipped your hand. Briggs is many things, but he's not stupid. And you wear your emotions on your sleeve."

"I almost had a heart attack. You realize this, right?" I lowered my hands and glared at him.

"Sorry." He winked at Lucy. She giggled.

Yeah, so not sorry. Demons. I shook my head.

"Go about your business!" Ethan hollered at the roost. "What's done is done. Everything's fine."

Everything's fine? I bristled.

Boos went up from among the crowd. Yeah, Ethan had way overstepped this time.

Ethan glared at them all. "Fuck off. I did what was best for the roost. I'm the Alpha. You don't like it, you can leave."

The crowd quieted, a low hum among the members. As if any of them had anywhere else to go. Leave their homes? Their roost? Not likely. But didn't mean they had to like it.

"That's what I thought." Ethan snarled and took a step toward the kids. While Lucy hadn't batted an eye at Briggs, she squeaked and darted behind my back. Jamie gripped my waist and buried his face in my chest.

"Don't make us go with him, Poe," Lucy said.

I tilted my chin up. Yeah, I'd take a beating for them. He wasn't getting them back. Not on my watch.

"So, it's like that, is it?" Ethan glared. He still sounded drunk. What a dumpster fire of a man. He took another step forward.

Tommy pursed his lips but kept quiet, though he placed a hand on Jamie's shoulder. But it wasn't Tommy's battle. He'd done enough.

"It's like that." I bared my teeth. "I'm taking the kids to school. They'll be staying with me. Go sleep it off, *Alpha*."

My blood boiled. It was on.

Ethan took another step closer, his fists clenched. The smell of stale bourbon wafted from his person. Had he showered in the damn stuff?

"No." Tommy didn't raise his voice, but Ethan froze.

He eyed Tommy like he'd only now noticed a demon in our midst. He opened his mouth, closed it with an audible clack. "Fuck you, boy," he said between gritted teeth. "You're out. Roostless."

I chuckled. Seriously?

"Oh, yeah? Who's gonna clean up your messes if I go? Who's gonna pay your debts?" I waited for the severing magic to strike. Didn't happen. That's what I thought.

Ethan spun and almost overbalanced. Could he be more pathetic? He marched off down the street toward his house. The roost moved aside for him but didn't disperse.

"You all can go home now or to work," I raised my voice, though it was suddenly so quiet you could have heard a pin drop. "I'm sorry for . . ." How did one apologize for that piece of shit? Instead, I waved in Ethan's general direction.

"You heard, Poe," Abe added. "Let's get going."

Several members waved before heading off.

"Damn, man, you've got balls," Abe called over his shoulder as he herded the stragglers away. "We need to talk. Later, Poe."

I waved. I had a lot of questions and things I wanted to say to Tommy, but now wasn't the right time. Coming here saved us, yet I'd have to answer to the roost for my deal. I'd hoped to keep it a secret. Stupid, I know. But more than that, I wanted to—

Tommy leaned up and placed his lips against mine in a soft caress. It was so unexpected that I froze. No one kissed me like I was . . . worth something. Hell, my hookups normally didn't even bother with the niceties. Before I could kiss him back, he'd retreated. Dammit.

"See you around, sugar. Stay away from Briggs." His gaze shot to the twins. "And the rest."

He didn't have to say "Ethan" for me to understand.

He strolled back to his limo, waved, and within seconds was gone. I just stood there like a dumbass.

"You should have kissed him back." Lucy tutted. "He likes you."

"Poe doesn't have much game," Jamie said to Lucy in all seriousness.

I rolled my eyes. "Wait until you guys are my age."

But they weren't wrong. At least where Tommy Tittoti was concerned, I had *zero* game.

12

The next morning, I dropped the kids off at school for the second day in a row, feeling lighter than I had in a long time. Something had shifted in our roost. Ethan hadn't been a popular alpha since before my mom died, but his signing over the twins' lives had further soured the relationship. Not that we could do fuck all about ousting him. But he'd planted the seeds of discord himself. If I had anything to say about it, we'd figure out a way to remove Ethan. One way or another.

Returning to Spun Gold, I was surprised to see the sign set to open. I cautiously peered in the window. Kennedy stood behind the counter having coffee with Abe. Huh. They both laughed, their heads together, Kennedy's hair brushing Abe's arm. Abe had tied his waist-length locs back into a loose ponytail at his nape and wore a fitted shirt that showed off his defined chest. Working on the docks had honed Abe's muscles in a way that being a gym rat never would. What was going on there? Harmless flirting, I'd guess. Kennedy had awful taste in guys. Even worse taste in ladies. Abe was way too nice for her.

Entering, I waved. Their conversation abruptly cut off, and they looked my way, the same exaggerated grin on their faces. Reminded me of some Stepford Wives shit.

"Hey," I said cautiously.

"Poe, my man," Abe pointed to a cup of coffee on the counter. "Join us."

Kennedy sniggered. "Yes, sweetie. Let's talk."

"Said the spider to the fly." But foolishly I went. I mean, coffee. I'm easy. The fresh grounds calling my name.

The coffee came from an actual café. Kennedy's doing, then. Who else could afford to spend $15 on a cup of real coffee and not the synthetic crap I drank daily? But oh, what a cup. I made a show of slurping noisily, and Kennedy wrinkled her nose. Abe hid a grin behind his hand.

"So what did you want to talk about?"

"We need a new alpha," Abe said, not mincing words.

"Yeah, agreed. But I've said as much since the dickhead became the roost alpha." I leaned against the counter. "As you've pointed out before. Doesn't work that way."

"Maybe it should." Kennedy's smile remained in place, but her eyes turned flinty.

"What? You want me to make him an offer he can't refuse?"

Neither laughed.

"Not *Godfather* fans, then?" I asked.

"Oh, was that what that was?" Kennedy smirked.

Abe coughed into his hand, looked away.

Fine. I wasn't an actor. Got it.

"Seriously, you two are freaking me out. What gives?"

Abe sighed. "Alpha is on a bad trajectory. We can all see it. I stopped by to visit him this morning. His house is littered with empty cans. Found him passed out on the couch. He'd smashed a bunch of dishes, put some new holes in the wall. He's not long for this world if things don't change."

As if we'd get so lucky.

"And what? You want me to get him into rehab?" I shook

my head. "He'd listen to anyone before me. Plus, I don't give a fuck if he crashes and burns as long as he doesn't take the roost with him."

"That's the point, hon. He very well may take the roost with him."

I sighed. Yeah, not news to me. "Okay, so what do you suggest?"

Abe shrugged, looking distinctly uncomfortable. Kennedy drew a finger across her throat. No wonder we were best friends. Still...

"I'm not a murderer." Sure, I thought about it a lot. And, yeah, in the heat of the moment, I could do it. But premeditated? Not really my thing. I ran more to thieving and avoiding confrontations.

"I wasn't talking about you." She gave me a significant look, like I should get what she meant.

Tommy? Was she crazy? I wouldn't bargain with him for Ethan's death. Besides, he'd as much as said he wouldn't deal with me again. Also, as much as I hated to admit it, I think that request would disappoint him. Not that I should care.

But I did.

I wasn't a good man. I wasn't a completely irredeemable one, either. Having someone else do my dirty work wasn't an option. But could I really free the roost from Ethan?

"We're not suggesting anything." Abe placed a workworn hand on my shoulder, his blunt nails digging in. "I just need you to prepare yourself." Again, another significant look.

Prepare myself? "I—"

The bell tinkled, and two potential customers came in. Abe stepped away.

"I'd better get to the docks. We can talk more about this

later."

Aaand another significant look. Abe nodded once, then strode from the shop like he was on a mission.

Kennedy shooed me away from the counter and gave the customers—a couple of older human women—her friendliest smile. Little did they know she'd squeeze every dime out of them.

"The newest items are in the front display case," she called to the women. "There's a couple of nice pendants."

"You're not even on until after lunch. I can handle the customers." Not that I wanted to, but it was *my* shop.

She rolled her eyes. "You need to go thank a certain demon for saving your ass yesterday."

I winced. "News travels fast."

"You could have texted me. I would have come with firepower." She glanced at her oversized Hermes handbag.

"Yeah, because that wouldn't have gotten roost territory razed to the ground."

"Well, maybe it would have encouraged Josephine Jones to get involved. I mean, what kind of Roger lets another infringe on her Neighborhood?" Kennedy's eyes went cold.

"One that doesn't want to go to war."

"Humph. Anyway, don't change subjects. You need to go thank him." Kennedy crossed her arms.

"You think?" My stomach did a little flip. Not cool. I shouldn't get so excited about the possibility of seeing him. I didn't *do* excited. Not when it came to guys.

"I'll be with you ladies in a moment," Kennedy called sweetly. Her smile fell away when she faced me. Her voice dropped. "Listen, Poe, pull your head out of your ass and go see Tommy. He took a big risk with you. The least you can do is tell him you appreciate it."

I swallowed. Well, I couldn't ignore my best friend's

advice, right? I nodded and gave her a quick hug.

As I left the shop, she called, "And don't forget the flowers!"

~

I FELT like an idiot strolling through Tommy's Neighborhood with a gigantic bouquet. I mean, who did that? I'd picked up the bunch from a flower shop at the corner of raven territory. Roses weren't cheap. But considering Tommy saved Lucy's life, I'd buy him ten bunches of flowers if it made him happy.

I stepped inside Rumpled Still, but Tommy was nowhere in sight. Carter raised a brow but pointed back toward the break room.

"He's in a crappy mood today, so enter at your own risk. Flowers, huh, rockstar?"

Should I go back? I could leave the flowers. If he was in a foul mood...

"Would you go on back? Gah, do you need me to write you an engraved invitation?" Carter typed away at the keyboard, glaring at me like I'd done something wrong.

Fine. I glared back, then headed toward the break room. Of course the door was closed. I knocked, quietly. You know, in case he was sleeping. Uh-huh. No nerves here.

"Come in," he snapped.

In for a penny... I pushed the door open, not sure what I would find.

Tommy curled up in the same oversized chair. He began to smile before his face took on a more neutral cast.

"Hey hot stuff, back to ask for another favor?" He kept his voice light, but he didn't fool me. He sounded disappointed.

And why would that be? I stuffed a hand in my jeans pocket and rocked back on my heels. Maybe coming here had been a mistake. I thrust the flowers at him. "No, I just wanted to thank you. I didn't properly say that yesterday morning, and you've been more than fair."

Tommy blinked. He tilted his head and seemed to consider my words. The silence stretched to awkward proportions.

I cleared my throat. "Okay then, I'm gonna go."

Tommy startled and grabbed the flowers. "No, I, you're welcome, sugar. It was a pleasure doing business with you. Among other things." This time he gave me a grin.

I couldn't tell whether he was mocking me or not. "I'm sure you say that to all the guys you lay in the back of your limo." I grinned back. Two could play at this. See? I could flirt. Sort of.

"Not all of them. You're definitely special." I don't know who looked more surprised by his words, me or him.

Did he mean them?

He breathed in the scent of the flowers before setting the bouquet on a side table.

"Aww, now you're just stroking my ego." I stepped forward until I leaned over him. I squatted so we were eye to eye. Time for a little honesty. "I mean it. You didn't have to give me such an easy bargain. The necklace was genius. Thank you." Chest fluttering, I leaned in and placed the softest kiss on his lips.

Just the slightest pressure of lip on lip, and my libido soared. I ignored it. I wasn't there to get laid.

As I pulled back, Tommy's hand wrapped around my nape. He tugged me closer and melded our mouths together. Fuck, he tasted good. His magic sparked around us, making my skin tingle.

We shouldn't do this. . . I hesitated. Screw it. I'd made worse decisions than to fuck around with a murder twink. I pressed closer. My fingers gripped Tommy's thighs and tugged him toward the end of the chair cushion, bringing our groins together. When I pulled back, Tommy groaned. I rested our foreheads together.

"I didn't come here for this, I swear."

"I know." He pushed my jacket off my shoulders and then tugged at my tee and pulled it over my head.

"Here?" I tried to sound scandalized, but honestly, I liked the thrill of getting caught. I didn't care who saw me. Never had.

Tommy chuckled as if he could read my mind. Before I could follow *that* train of thought, he reached for the waist of my jeans. I batted his hand away and stood up. I slowly undid the button and lowered the zipper.

"Tease." Tommy scrambled to his knees and threw off his shirt, unfastened and shimmied out of his jeans. He wore a hot pink jockstrap with the words "The Boss" on the waistband.

I whistled.

He turned around in the chair, offering me his glorious ass. I groaned. I preferred to bottom, but I enjoyed topping almost as much. Especially when said ass bounced when I slapped it. Tommy growled. The predator letting me know my place. My dick was so onboard with this. Hair rose on my arms. All right, then.

I placed my hands on Tommy's hips pulling him toward the edge of the chair. I swore under my breath.

"I don't have any lube. I don't suppose there's any here?"

Tommy snapped his fingers. A bottle appeared in his hand. He handed it back to me, and I quickly slid my jeans and underwear down, then slicked myself up. Him naked and me fully clothed seemed to be a thing. I liked it. A lot. I pushed two slick fingers between his cheeks and against his pucker. Rested them there.

"Get on with it, birdie." Shimmers surrounded us, his energy snapping.

"Just seeing if you really are the boss. Somehow I'm not surprised." I laughed, feeling happy for the first time in a while.

Before Tommy could retort, I slid my fingers deep. I wasn't gentle, though I didn't try to hurt him, either. Tommy spread his legs wider to give me room to work. I moved my fingers in and out for a moment and then added a third, then a fourth finger. Before he could complain, I removed my fingers, lined up, and slid in deep. One thrust. Balls deep. Shivered, holding myself as still as possible. Perfection.

I waited for Tommy to adjust and then slowly withdrew, only to push back to the hilt. The angle was divine. Tommy seemed to think so, too, if his growls were a sign. A bird could get used to this.

My pace gradually increased, his heat driving me crazy. The sound of our bodies slapping had to be audible down the hallway. I didn't give a fuck. On second thought, I supposed I did.

I slid my hand around and into his jock. I gripped Tommy's dick. For a little guy, he was well-endowed. Figured. Uncut, too. And he was so hard. The tip wet. Damn, he felt so good both in my hand and wrapped around my cock.

"Fuck," I said. "So hot. So fucking hot." Apparently I had forgotten how to talk. I babbled more nonsense, my other hand digging into his hip to hold him in place. I stroked him in time with my thrusts, even added a twist on the downstroke using his foreskin to aid in the pleasure. I might not be all that old compared with Tommy, but I'd used my time on Earth well.

His body tightened, and it was all I could do to hold on. My pace sped, and Tommy threw his head back, resting it on my shoulder. He was so beautiful, his long lashes sweeping his cheeks as he rocked back on my cock. I kissed the pulse at the base of his neck, and he arched like I'd electrocuted him. Come shot from his cock and coated my fingers, and his ass clamped down on me, shoving me over the edge. My orgasm barreled through me, and I clasped him to me as I filled him up.

Once I'd caught my breath, I released my death grip and eased out. He didn't turn around. I watched my spunk run down his thigh and I had the urge to lap it up.

I didn't.

I righted my jeans and underwear, then grabbed my tee and jacket. Tommy stayed in the same position.

"Everything all right?" I went to touch his shoulder, but he flinched away. Had I hurt him? "Tommy?"

"Thanks for a good time, sugar." He turned to face me. His eyes had returned to their normal shade, and his face was closed off. "You're a good lay. It's a pleasant way to conclude our business arrangement."

The unexpected sting of his words had me taking a step back. I'd thought. . . Oh. I knew this dance a little too well. Dismissed. "Yeah, glad I could oblige."

"You did. We had fun, birdie. Let's leave it at that."

"Flowers and a lay. Service with a smile." I gave him my best smirk. "Anyway, I'll see you around."

"The plan is that you don't." Tommy's cheek twitched.

"Don't worry, I know when my welcome's worn out. I'll see myself out." I nodded, and turning, opened the door and walked out. I didn't look back.

13

It had been over two weeks since I last spoke to Tommy. Not that I was counting. I didn't even think about him. Except on Sundays. And sometimes other days of the week. Not even sure why. It wasn't like we had anything special. Or anything at all. Just a business arrangement, like he said.

Another Sunday. I stood outside the community center waiting for his people to show up. He never came. But I'd gotten to know a few of them—like Ruston, the rangy wolf Jamie had taken a shine to. They always teamed up for dodgeball, and Lucy schooled them each week. But they kept trying.

I leaned against the wall, the coolness of the day making me glad I wore my leather jacket. My nose itched from the smell of decaying leaves and mold spores in the air. Not that we had an abundance of vegetation in our few blocks, but we tried. A few anemic trees survived in square plots along the sidewalk and we'd planted mums near the community center entrance.

It had been quiet. I couldn't bring myself to ask any of Tommy's people about him.

Nothing from Briggs, either.

And I hadn't seen Ethan since the blood debt incident.

The twins stayed with me, and I had no plans to return them.

Kennedy kept side-eyeing me for the last week or so, but she didn't say anything. I'd asked her to look for another heist for me. Not in Briggs' Neighborhood. That was a no-go. I'd take the job in any other area of Baltimore. So far, she hadn't come through.

Not gonna lie. Abe stopping by every day to shoot the shit freaked me out a bit. Only Ollie seemed normal. Or what passed for normal for him.

An air of expectation hung over our streets. For what, I wasn't sure. But like Tommy's magic, I could almost feel the crackle in the air.

"Boy," Ethan's voice cut through my thoughts.

I *had* to jinx myself. I steeled my spine, turned toward his voice. Not giving the twins up without a fight.

My stepdad's appearance had me raising my eyebrows. A new suit and shoes, his face freshly shaven, and were those lipstick marks on his cheeks? His rolling gait told me he'd been on a binger, but his eyes looked bright, and his cocky grin didn't bode well for me. Most disconcerting, he wore a large snakehead badge on his lapel.

I decided to keep quiet. Naturally, I did that by saying, "What the fuck do you want?"

"Don't talk to me that way, boy. I've got important news."

"What news?"

"Briggs Bickley made me one of his lieutenants." Ethan tapped the snakehead badge.

"I wouldn't think Josephine Jones would allow that with our area being in her Neighborhood."

"She doesn't get a say. Besides, Mister Bickley explained his plan for Baltimore. He's a real visionary."

That word again. Briggs was many things. Greedy. Selfish. But visionary? Nah.

"Okay, why are you telling me?" I crossed my arms. Nothing good could come from this. We didn't need to be in the middle of two quarreling Rogers.

"I want you to sell your shop and the community center to Mister Bickley."

I laughed. "Fuck off. You don't get a say in what I do with my property." Not to mention, Tommy now owned 51 percent of Spun Gold Jewelers.

"He's going to turn this area into another casino. Your buildings need to go."

"Just my businesses? How's that gonna work?" The moment I said it, my chest squeezed tight.

He didn't.

He wouldn't.

Ethan reached into his suit coat and pulled out a contract. "I signed over all the other territory. Don't need it. He'll be moving the roost into some new housing. He's petitioned MASC to allow the building permits. Jones won't have a lot of choice. It might be her Neighborhood, but it's not her land to sell."

"It wasn't yours to sell, either," I snarled. "You had no right. That land belongs to the roost!"

"I *am* the roost. And you better learn it now, boy." Ethan grabbed me and slammed me against the wall.

My collarbone snapped. I gasped from the pain.

"You listen here—" he began.

"How could you do this? This is *our territory*." I shoved Ethan away from me with my good arm. Territory was *everything*.

"You don't have to be part of this roost if you don't like the way I run things."

"What roost? You left everyone homeless, you selfish fuck. There *is* no roost."

I saw it coming but didn't have time to duck. Ethan didn't pull his punch. I slammed back into the wall but came up swinging. It might be hopeless, but Ethan didn't deserve to walk away from this pain-free. I connected with his jaw, and it felt like punching the wall. Probably broke my hand. Ethan swung at me again and again, boxing me in. A well-aimed kick to my knee brought me to the ground. Still, I fought.

"You always were a stubborn one. Here's what you're gonna do. You're gonna sign over your little shop and the community center. You're gonna watch your mouth and be thankful you'll have a place with the roost. I might even let you keep the twins. *If* you behave. And you're gonna be real nice to Mister Bickley. Real nice."

My head spun. My mouth filled with blood from biting my tongue when I fell. I spat it out on his new shiny shoes. "Fuck. You."

Ethan kicked me again.

"Alpha! What are you doing? Stop!" Abe's voice sounded like it came from a long tunnel.

I curled into a ball to protect myself. Ethan's kicks kept coming.

"Alpha—" Abe grunted and fell on top of me. Ethan had slugged him, too. "You'll kill him!" Abe gasped out.

"And what if I do? Who's gonna stop me?"

The pulling back of the slide on a pistol was surprisingly loud with all the commotion.

I cracked an eye open. Kennedy stood behind Ethan with a brand new Glock 52 pressed to the back of his skull. Her lip had pulled back in a snarl, and her eyes blazed with fury. "I will. Gladly."

Ethan froze, his face gone white. She meant it. He knew it. I knew it. He held up his hands in front of him but didn't say a thing.

"Abe, take Poe inside. Alpha Short and I are overdue to have a little talk." Kennedy's cheeks had flushed scarlet, and she held the Glock nice and steady.

I wanted to protest, but couldn't do much more than whimper when Abe stood and lifted me like a baby. The most grievous wounds were healing—painfully—but it would take time for my body to set itself to rights.

As everything faded out, I knew a visit to Tommy Tittoti was in my future.

∼

KENNEDY HADN'T KILLED my piece of shit stepdad. She refused to tell me what she'd said to him. Abe hovered around trying to nursemaid me in the community center's back office. He'd laid me out on a pile of gym mats. Luckily the twins hadn't noticed our entrance, too caught up in their games, and Abe had avoided the gym area.

"If you'd let me take you to the hospital, they could treat your injuries faster," Abe said for the hundredth time. Like I had money for an ER visit. The roost would need every dime.

"I'll be fine." And I would. Just not quite yet. I painstakingly pushed myself to sitting, biting my lip not to whimper. He'd done a number on me this time. "I need to see Tommy."

"No way!" Abe paced the small office. "You shouldn't have dealt with him in the first place. The guy's dangerous. Kennedy said he's already done you two favors. Three's the lucky number, right, Kennedy?"

Kennedy pursed her lips, pulled out her cell. "You should go. The kids can come home with me for the night. Here, I'll order you a ride."

"You can't be serious." Abe stopped in front of her. "Look at him. He can't even stand on his own."

"Dead serious." Kennedy tapped her screen. "You heard what Poe said. Ethan signed away your home and the rest of the roost's, too. Where do you think Briggs will put you guys once he has you out of the way? He's not giving you primo housing. You'll be lucky to get anything. He doesn't need the roost now that he has your land. Ethan's a fool."

Kennedy and Abe argued until her phone beeped. My ride had arrived.

～

THAT'S how early that afternoon I found myself slinking into Rumpled Still. If I'd been a dog, I would have had my tail between my legs. The barber shop smelled of shaving cream and that spicy aftershave Tommy had used on me. My eyes watered. Every step hurt.

Tommy chatted animatedly with an older mage as he trimmed the guy's wiry beard. The glow surrounding them kept sound from carrying. I could see Tommy's lips move, but I couldn't hear what he said.

When Tommy looked up and met my gaze, his lips thinned, and his eyes shifted to red. He broke the contact and nodded toward the front desk. I limped over, and Carter whistled. "You look like you've been run over. Twice."

When I simply nodded, Carter frowned.

"Have a seat, rockstar. Tommy will be with you when he can." Carter came from around the desk and awkwardly offered me his arm for support. I appreciated the gesture but had too much pride to take it.

Instead, I forced myself to stand up straighter and walk as if I weren't in agony. If I had to grit my teeth and bite my tongue not to scream, so be it.

I sank down into the offered chair and almost moaned at how good it felt to be off my feet. My ribs were healing, but between the collarbone and the other damage, it would take some time. And bones always healed before tissue. I hoped Ethan hadn't punctured a lung, because breathing wasn't the easiest right now. Maybe I should have waited to come... but patience wasn't one of my virtues.

Carter came back with some ice in a towel and gently placed it over my swollen cheek and eye. I reached out to grab the icepack. Sucked in a harsh breath from the pain it caused to lift my arm.

"I got it. Just relax." Carter kept his hand in place and didn't ask questions. I was grateful. My breathing wasn't getting any easier, though.

"Hey, sugar," a familiar honeyed voice said. I hadn't even heard Tommy approach. Hadn't noticed that the mage had left. "Carter and I are going to help you to the break room. I need you to lie down, so I can examine you. You don't look so good."

I did my best to grin. "Are you trying to say I look like shit?"

"Warmed over and served on a platter. Come on, birdie."

It hurt like hell when they pulled me to my feet. I staggered. Whatever adrenaline had carried me here had long since fled. I sagged toward the floor, but they kept me upright. I'd be mortified, except it was everything I could do to draw breath.

Next thing I knew, my world tilted, and I found myself

on my back on the teal velveteen sofa in the break room. Carter laid the icepack back on my eye socket. "Do you want me to stay, Bossman?"

"No, thank you, Carter. I have this."

Carter nodded, and a moment later I heard the door close but couldn't turn my head to check.

Tommy eased my tee up my chest. He growled. Guess I was pretty bruised up. "Please tell me you've come to ask that I eliminate your stepdad. I'll give you an excellent deal. I'm assuming he's the one that did this."

"Guessed it in one." I tried to chuckle, but it hurt too much. I groaned instead.

"Hold still. You're going to feel a little heat." Tommy placed his hands on my chest and belly. "You're lucky I have a mark coming in to pay her debt, or I wouldn't be able to do this."

If it wasn't so painful, I would've enjoyed his touch. Heat radiated from Tommy's hands. I groaned. Fire spread through my body. It hurt. But I didn't have control of my limbs to do anything about it.

"Shhh, it's okay. I'm almost done." Tommy continued, his face scrunched up in concentration. The heat dissipated.

I sucked in a great breath of air. My body felt heavy as my eyelids drooped. Tommy ran a gentle hand through my hair. "Sleep a bit. I'll be back to check on you after my next client."

He stood up, and I tried to reach for his hand, but my body wouldn't cooperate. Tommy placed a quilt over me and intoned, "Sleep."

I did.

14

Waking up took effort. Grit stuck my lids together, and blackness called. I ignored it. Cracked my eyes open. Tommy sat next to me on the sofa.

He ran a hand through my hair. "Hi there."

"Hi. How long have I been asleep?"

"About 6 hours."

Whoa. Felt like only moments.

"I didn't mean to pass out on you." I rubbed a hand over my face as if I could wipe away the stress and worry. Thank God, Kennedy had the kids for the night.

"You needed it." Tommy looked down at his hands. "What happened, Poe?"

My jaw firmed. "Ethan signed away everything. Briggs dangled a lieutenant-ship, and he just rolled over and showed his belly. There's only the community center and my shop left now. And that's only because I own them outright. Though Ethan is demanding I sell to Briggs."

"And he used you as his personal punching bag to get what he wants." Tommy kept his voice light, but I could feel the angry energy crackling around him. That was . . . unexpected.

"I had a few things to say to him." I frowned. "No way I'm selling to Briggs."

Tommy leaned back, nodded. "Jos is going to be livid when she hears what your stepdad did."

"She'll fight him for it?" She had done nothing so far, but maybe now she'd have to act.

"If I had to guess, she'll ask MASC for a hearing. A commission with the five Rogers and a MASC representative."

"Will she be able to stop him?"

Tommy shrugged. "Possibly."

"But you're not sure."

"No." Tommy raised an eyebrow. "So then, Poe, what brings you to my doorstep?"

I noticeably swallowed and averted my eyes. I didn't want to ask him for anything more. He'd as much as told me to fuck off. But I couldn't do it without him. "I need help to get the roost's territory back."

Tommy shook his head. "The roost is not your concern anymore."

I glared. "Ethan didn't sever my bond to the roost. He likes to threaten it, but he doesn't dare. So, they'll always be my concern."

"It seems to me, birdie, you're caring for everyone else, but who's caring for you?"

I sat up and raked an angry hand through my hair. "I don't need anyone to look after me. They do."

Tommy cocked his head. "If that were true, you wouldn't be here. They would. But here you are. And it's not too much of a leap to expect that you want another bargain."

I blew out a frustrated breath. "I don't *want* another bargain. I just don't feel as if I have a choice."

"You do. Walk away, sugar."

"You don't understand because you're not a shifter. We're

pack animals. I don't know what demons are, but I doubt you feel unfulfilled without other demons."

Tommy tapped his chin. "You're right there."

"We also value territory. Those blocks have been in our roost for generations."

"Now, *that* I do understand."

"So you'll help me?" I tried not to sound too pathetic.

"I can't." His lips thinned, and he squeezed my bicep.

"Can't? Or won't?"

"It's one and the same, sugar. Briggs would never give me an opportunity to bargain for the territory. And without a bargain, I can't get it back."

I sagged, my head in my hands. "It's my fault."

Tommy snorted inelegantly. "And how, pray tell, is this your fault? You didn't sign away your territory."

"Briggs said he'd keep taking things away until I gave into him."

"Your skill set would be very useful to him." Tommy's voice came out monotone, not a hint of feeling—good or bad—behind it.

I growled. "It's not just my skills he wants."

"Sugar, Briggs is making a power play. Your roost, and you, more specifically, are casualties of that."

"Fuck."

"Well, he'll certainly expect it." Tommy huffed.

"Real funny." I moved my shoulder, placed a hand on my collarbone. "You fixed it."

"I did."

"Why?"

Tommy focused on my collarbone. "I could hardly find out what you wanted if you stayed passed out from the pain. Seemed faster to get what I wanted."

Not even slightly convincing. "I don't believe you."

Tommy bared his fangs. "I'm not a nice guy, Poe. Don't turn me into something I'm not."

My hand came to his cheek. "I think you're nicer than you pretend."

When I leaned in until our mouths were inches from each other, Tommy didn't pull away. So, I pressed my lips gently to his.

Tommy moaned deep into the kiss.

Even after being banged up, just a touch and I was ready to go. One kiss turned into several. When we finally broke for air, I found Tommy on my lap. He'd extended his claws. One hand gripped my hair in a too-tight hold. The other rested against my cheek. He tipped my head back, holding me in a pose that bared my neck. A sign of submission in wolves. Ravens didn't buy into that posturing crap.

Instead, I trembled. And not in fear. Tommy's pupils were blown, and his lips kiss swollen. When I tried to move, he growled at me, and it sent lightning zinging through my system. He bit his bottom lip, his gaze scanning my face. He slowly let go, then slid off my lap.

"What—"

"You came here for business." Tommy's eyes still glowed a fiery red. He took a deep breath. "So let's deal."

"You said you couldn't help."

"Oh, sugar, I never said that. I said I couldn't get your roost's territory back."

I crossed my arms. "So what exactly are you offering?"

"Same deal as Briggs. Only I promise, I'll take better care of you."

I scooted away from Tommy. "What the fuck? I'm not for sale."

Tommy leered. "Aren't you? What other choice do you

have? You say you want to save your roost. I'll give you a way. If I end up with your roost, too, well, it's a good deal for me." He shrugged, as if he wasn't talking about my life and people I cared about. "But see, unlike Briggs, I'm a fair demon. Willing to make you a deal. You know I'll keep it. Are you saying that you don't want it?" His voice held a note of challenge.

Heat burned the back of my neck, and my ears felt hot. My fists clenched. "Is this what you've been working toward the whole time?"

"What did you think? I keep telling you, I'm a demon. It's what we do. It's not my fault you won't listen."

Humiliation sank its claws deep. Except, he almost seemed *too* casual about it. What was he playing at? One way to find out.

I shot to my feet. "I'd be better off in Briggs' bed. At least I know what I'm getting there. I might as well go get it over with."

I stormed to the door and threw it open. It slammed against the wall with a bang.

"Poe, wait!" Tommy's voice came out more growl than words.

I spun around and pointed. "Ha! I fucking knew it."

He looked like a kid with his hand caught in the cookie jar. "I was just going to say ... good luck."

I swaggered back to him. "You don't fool me, Tommy Tittoti. You don't want to see me in Briggs' bed any more than I want to be there."

Color rose in Tommy's face. "No, of course not. What a waste."

"Fuck off. You're trying to scare me away."

"And what if I am? You need to think of yourself."

I squatted so that we were nose to nose. "I think you like

that I care about others. Somewhere in that shriveled demon's heart of yours, you care, too."

Tommy scoffed. "You're being overly generous with my character, shug."

"I want you to help me get my roost's territory back. I'm willing to give you what you asked for if you do."

Tommy growled. "No. I told you. The blocks are a lost cause."

"Then help me find new ones for the roost."

"My price is too high."

"Tell me what it is, and I'll pay it." I reached for the bottom of my tee and pulled it off. If he didn't think I was serious, he had another think coming. I ran a hand down my stomach and slipped it beneath the waistband of my jeans.

"What are you doing?" Tommy licked his lips.

"Giving you a free sample."

"Poe, I . . . can't. Not like this. I'm not a rapist." He shook his head, his eyes still glowing red, his fingers dug into the couch.

He wanted me.

At least for now.

I withdrew my hand but stood and unbuttoned and unzipped my jeans. I shoved both my underwear and pants down my thighs to pool at my ankles. Stepped out of them. I stood completely naked in front of him. "It's not rape if I'm willing."

His eyes glowed brighter. "I wouldn't ask you to bargain with your body. Even *I* have standards."

"I thought incubi were all about sex?"

"Incubi? Where did you get that idea?" He chuckled. "No, sugar, I'm more your garden-variety imp. They wouldn't allow me to remain in this world if I could suck creatures' souls dry through sex."

"You make an excellent point."

Tommy ran a hand over his face. He suddenly looked tired. "Get dressed, and we'll talk."

Instead, I sat down next to him. I leaned over and whispered in his ear, "Let's talk later. I'm already naked, so I think we should have some fun first."

"Shug, I'm trying to do the right thing here. I don't want to take advantage of your situation."

"Isn't that what you said demons do?"

"Not over something like this." He inched away, but I closed the gap between us.

"This has nothing to do with business. Your conscience will be clear."

"And if I refuse to help you afterward? Won't you have regrets? Feel used?" Tommy shook his head. "I like you, sugar. It's rare I get a decent man asking me for help. You don't even ask for yourself. You have no idea how unusual that is. So, I don't want that between us. Let me do the right thing. For once."

I sighed but grudgingly pulled on my clothing. I shouldn't feel rejected.

Just sex, after all.

Ha! Even I didn't believe my bullshit. Once fully dressed, I leaned back on the sofa, my arms crossed. No, I wasn't pouting.

"You're pouting." Tommy's lips turned up in the hint of a smug smile.

Not worth the energy to deny it. Instead, I shrugged.

"Oh, shug, you really are something." Tommy grasped my bicep and tugged me to him. He kissed me.

The familiar electricity shot through my limbs. How did he do that? I'd have to ask him sometime, except at the moment I was too busy letting him tongue fuck my mouth. I'd never been with a guy who liked kissing as much as he did. And he was a master. It was stupid to say I felt like a virgin—that ship sailed long ago—but his kisses made me feel desired. Cherished even. Guess that spoke to the quality of the guys I usually hooked up with when a murder twink set the bar.

His tongue stroked against mine, and I melted against the couch, my body boneless as he manhandled me, coming down on top.

"You are so responsive, birdie." Tommy groaned against my lips. "You tempt a demon."

"We all have our talents," I said between kisses. Mine apparently ran to tempting dangerous creatures. In his case, I didn't mind.

"Damn you, Poe Dupin." Tommy slithered down my body and tore at my jeans. Looked like I'd pushed him too far. I lifted my hips to help him get my jeans and underwear off. He only pulled them to my thighs before his mouth engulfed my cock in wet heat. Oh, fuck, that felt glorious.

Tommy didn't tease. He wrapped his lips around me and set up a fast glide, his other hand cupping my balls. His magic sparked and made my nerve endings even more sensitive. Shit!

"You need to stop, or it's gonna be over before it's started."

The damn demon doubled down. A hand clamped onto my hip in a bruising grip, holding me exactly where he wanted. I bucked into his mouth. He took it all, his nose pressed into my trimmed thatch of hair. Of course a demon didn't have a gag reflex.

He didn't let up, the suction just this side of blinding

pleasure. At a particularly aggressive slide, I let out a whine that I didn't even know I could make. But here we were.

Tommy smiled around my length, satisfaction writ large on his face. The smell of apples flooded my senses, and I gasped. I wanted to wrap myself in his smell, wear it like a blanket. I wanted—

I gripped his hair, not to control him, but to have something to hang onto because I could swear he was sucking my soul—and definitely my brains—out through my cock. Was he sure he wasn't an incubus? Holy fuck.

"So close," I gasped out, my voice wrecked.

Our gazes met. His, hot and possessive. No mistaking that. I should have been horrified. Instead, my balls pulled up tight, my back arched, and I fought to breathe as he violently shoved me over the edge.

I came down his throat, my stomach muscles contracting. Pretty sure I shouted loud enough for the whole block to hear. My thighs shook, and my limbs spasmed before going limp. I let out a heartfelt groan of approval.

Tommy pulled off and licked me clean before tucking me back into my jeans.

I panted, my nerves still sizzling. "Give me a minute, and I'll return the favor."

"No need. That was for you." He sighed, his head resting on my thigh. "This doesn't change anything, you know."

"Yeah, it does." I couldn't exactly say what. But I knew it did.

Tommy grimaced. "Fine. But you still shouldn't be bargaining with me."

"Okay."

"Okay?" Tommy's face showed his disbelief.

"Yeah, I get it."

"You do?"

"Don't sound so surprised. I appreciate that you don't want to take advantage of me. If you can't get our territory back, I'll have to figure out another way."

Tommy pushed up so we were nose to nose. "Don't you dare fall into Briggs' bed. He won't treat you well."

I snorted. "I'm not falling into his bed."

"So what *do* you plan to do?"

"Me? Keep my employees working. I'm thinking I may have to take over the community center for the roost so they have at least a temporary place to stay. Running water, showers, basic kitchen. No way Briggs is gonna provide them with safe housing. I can put their mattresses and things into the gym area. Your people can still come by and use the pool and some other facilities on Sundays, but the gym may be closed for a bit."

"And what about your stepdad? Are you willing to let him stay there?"

I growled. "Fuck no. He can go sleep at the end of Briggs' bed. I'm not letting him near the twins."

"That's what I thought." Tommy shifted against me, his compact bulk surprisingly solid.

"You have any better ideas?"

"You mean other than killing him?"

I barked out a laugh. "Yeah, demon, other than killing him."

"You could stage a coup."

"And how would I do that? I told you, I can't best him in a head-on competition. He can draw on the rest of the roost for strength. Including mine. You saw what he did to me."

Tommy frowned. "Don't remind me."

"Awww, you care." I said it like I was joking, but it actually touched me that Tommy seemed to. Maybe I was naïve.

Tommy sighed again. "You're okay. For a bird."

"All this flattery will go to my head."

Tommy chuckled, and then he pursed his lips and narrowed his eyes.

"What?" I traced Tommy's jawline with a finger. He was so damn sexy.

"I have a solution, and it doesn't even require you to make a deal with me."

He had my attention. "Oh?"

Tommy pushed himself a little higher on my chest. "You offer to let them join your roost instead. You have your own territory. The community center and Spun Gold are enough, right? It's not much to begin with, but I bet it will be enough for some of your roost. Especially since Ethan Short has left them all homeless. I'm guessing you'll find several families receptive."

Now that was an interesting plan. Before they had their homes and their businesses to lose if they followed me. But now... "That's diabolical."

"Well, I am a demon. We do diabolical well."

"It doesn't solve the problem with Lucy and Jamie. He's still their dad."

"Let him bring the issue to Josephine Jones. Your territory is still in her Neighborhood, whatever your stepdad likes to pretend. See how likely she is to give him the kids back after he sold three blocks of her Neighborhood to Briggs."

"That could work." My heart beat faster. No way she'd give him the twins. If nothing else, Rogers could be hella spiteful. And Jones had every reason to be.

"Okay, then why do you look so pensive? This should be good news, right?"

"I don't know that I'm alpha material." I hadn't considered it before. Ravens didn't have natural casts like wolves.

We weren't born to be a beta or alpha or whatever. I always assumed one of Ethan's betas would step into that role if something happened to him. Normally, the roost chose the alpha. But I was setting it up so that I would be alpha by default. A genius workaround. Would my roost accept it? Accept me?

Tommy placed his head back down on my chest and traced a finger across my collarbone. "That's what will make you a good one, birdie. You'll work to deserve it."

"You think?"

"I know."

"Okay, I'll do it."

15

Tommy had generously lent me his limo. I could have easily walked back home, but he insisted, and I didn't resist. I had plans to make. Michael wasn't driving this time, but Finch—another wolf shifter—was chatty. Seemed he enjoyed working for Tommy. He'd become a lone wolf from one of the North Carolina packs when his brother took over and decided he threatened the new order. I winced in sympathy. Wolves were even more reliant on packs than ravens. His story sounded like Ruston's. I'd have to ask Michael for his story sometime. Seemed Tommy was a collector of damaged goods. Maybe that's why he helped me, too.

As the limo turned onto my block, we were met by chaos. My street was awash in sirens and strobing lights. Fire engines lined the avenue, and firefighters fought large blazes. An ambulance roared up to the area near where Spun Gold stood.

"Stop the car!" I was already hopping out by the time the limo began to brake. I sprinted toward my business, then skidded to a halt. My shop sat in a smoldering ruin. Firefighters still worked on stray bits of flame, but they had the fire under control.

The building and the one next to it were total losses. What the hell happened? I was pretty sure I already knew the answer. Before my rage could bubble over, I noticed the EMTs on the scene. Had someone been hurt?

The EMTs hurriedly lifted someone onto a stretcher—toward the ambulance. I pushed my way over and recognized Ollie's still form being loaded into the vehicle.

"Excuse me, I'm his boss. What happened to him? Is he okay?"

"We're headed to Butcher's Hill. You can find out more there." An EMT crawled in behind the stretcher and pulled the door closed. The ambulance shot off into the night.

Fuck. Butcher's Hill was technically the closest shifter hospital. But it had earned its name. To add insult to injury, it sat only a stone's throw from one of the best hospitals in the country.

I scanned the firefighters. I knew several of them from hanging out at one of their bars. Had hooked up with more than one. All were currently busy with the flames. While not every wall had collapsed, I could see enough to know that someone had also stolen my safe. Greedy fuckers. Good thing I hadn't kept much in it.

Members of my roost lingered in their doorways, looking scared. Did they know they'd soon be homeless? Had Ethan told them? Had Abe?

Another fire blazed farther down the block. I had a sneaking suspicion I knew what building was on fire. I jogged that way. Sure enough, flames engulfed the community center. Silver streams of water fought the fire, but it still burned hot.

"Poe!" One firefighter called, lifting her visor. She hurried my way. Ash darkened her cheeks, but I recognized her. She'd kicked my ass at pool on more than one occasion.

"Alejandra, what happened?"

"We received a call of several fires in your area. I recognized your shop. Is this your roost's?"

"No, it's also mine. Please tell me no one was in the community center. It should have been closed, but staff sometimes stay late to clean or play a game of pick-up."

"We didn't find anyone."

"Any witnesses to who set it?"

Alejandra frowned. "We haven't declared it arson. Yet."

"Come on. You know this couldn't be coincidence."

Her face closed down. "You're going to have to talk to the fire marshal. She's good at her job. She'll have more information for you once we get this blaze under control. And she's able to sort through the wreckage. Accelerants have obvious patterns to the burn. She'll have some questions for you."

I nodded, suddenly numb. Did she think I'd done this? Fuck. "The fire injured one of my employees. I need to check on him. Thanks for telling me what you know."

"You got it." She slapped me on the shoulder before jogging off toward an engine.

I sent off a quick text to Kennedy to make sure the twins were safe. I didn't mention the fire. No reason to worry her, too.

Could this night get any worse?

16

Ollie rested under heavy sedation in the ICU. He'd suffered head trauma, burns over eighty percent of his body, and had inhaled a lot of smoke. He could only breathe with the aid of a ventilator. A grim prognosis.

A nurse had let it slip that he'd been set on fire. Not caught on fire. Set. My stomach roiled. He hadn't deserved that. Hadn't deserved any of it.

I paced the small ICU waiting room at Butcher's Hill, the smell of antiseptic and sweat overpowering. I could rebuild my business. Same couldn't be said of Ollie. I should have sent the kid home. When I'd refused to sell, I should have expected a swift reaction. I gripped my hair tight, the pain grounding.

He couldn't die. My fault. I knew better than anyone how dangerous Briggs could be. Maybe Tommy could . . . No, he'd been clear. No more deals.

Ollie's parents had showed up an hour ago and talked with the doctor in charge of his treatment. Beth towered over Terry and the doctor, but what Terry lacked in height, he made up for in breadth. Stocky with a graying, close-trimmed beard, he gave Ollie his tightly curled hair and his height, if not his bulk. Instead, Ollie had a slender build like his mom and her fine features.

They were in with Ollie now. They'd had to suit up fully to keep the possibility of infection at bay. Shifters healed better than humans, but even we had our limits.

Set on fire. Fuck.

I paced the room again, wearing a path across the faded blue carpet. Two rows of pleather chairs in an equally faded leopard print sat in a corner of the room. A large blue, green, and yellow abstract painting took up most of one wall. It reminded me of the ocean. Guess that was the point. Soothing.

A hard-faced attendant sitting at a large metal desk behind a plexiglass enclosure kept me from sneaking past to check on Ollie. That, and you had to be buzzed in. Sure, I could pick the lock, but not while she watched.

They wouldn't allow me to see him. Only family.

Ollie's parents stepped back into the waiting room. Beth had tears streaming down her face, and Terry looked like he'd aged ten years. I tensed, expecting the worst.

Ollie's mom came straight my way and threw her arms around me. I stood stock still for a second before wrapping her up and hugging her back. "I'm so sorry, Beth. If I could've taken his place, I would."

"Don't say such things, Poe." She held on. A snuffle escaped, then a sob. "They don't think he's going to make it through the night."

My gut felt like Ethan had punched me. No, no, no. I looked to Terry, and he nodded confirmation.

Beth's sobbing grew louder. Terry and I helped her over to a pleather chair, and each sat on one side of her.

Beth gripped our hands tight enough to cut off the blood flow. "We haven't been fair to him, you know. We were so proud when he went off to that fancy school. With humans, even. And then the car theft. We knew it wasn't his idea, that we taught him better than that. I haven't told you, Poe, but I was grateful you gave him a job when others turned their backs on us. On him. He's a good kid."

"Yeah, he is. The best." Tears prickled my eyes.

"He looks up to you."

Me? A first-rate thief? Hardly the role model for Ollie—or anyone. "I let him down."

Beth laughed. It came out slightly hysterical, and she released her husband's fingers to clamp a hand over her mouth. After she gained control, she swallowed. "We all let him down. Everyone, *except* you."

I shook my head. "I think Briggs Bickley did this as revenge. I shouldn't have let Ollie keep working, knowing that Briggs might come after me. Or those I care about."

She seemed to consider my answer, fresh tears making tracks down her cheeks. Then she squeezed my hand. "We can't control the pain that others cause, we can only try to minimize the damage we ourselves do. I wish we'd been better to Ollie when he came home. I wish we'd let him know that we love him and just want him to be happy. Looks like we won't get that chance."

I squeezed her hand back. We sat in silence for a while, me steeping in my guilt. Why couldn't I have—

Beth cleared her throat. "Do you know what the plan is now that our alpha—" she said the words with all the derision she could muster, "—sold our homes and businesses?"

News traveled fast.

"Ethan said Briggs is gonna provide us lodging. Ethan believes he'll become important to Briggs Bickley now."

Beth snorted. "What about Roger Jones? I can't imagine she's okay with him carving away part of her Neighborhood."

I shrugged. I wouldn't mention my plan, now that it

wasn't possible. "I have some money saved if we need it. We'll figure something out."

Beth patted me on the knee. "As much as I hate to say it, you're better off without the roost. You've provided jobs, given money, and paid many of our protection fees. You could start over. Leave us in the rearview mirror."

"And what about you all? How are you supposed to get by? Besides, I'm born and bred Baltimore. Just because my business burned down doesn't mean I'm throwing in the towel. I have insurance. I'll rebuild. Or use the money to buy a new place. I'll still employ as many ravens as I'm able."

Terry nodded toward the doorway. "He a friend of yours? He keeps looking over at us."

I glanced that way. Tommy Tittoti stood just inside the waiting room, looking uncertain, his hands shoved in his hoodie's pockets.

"Tommy!" I shot to my feet and hurried over. "What are you doing here?"

"I heard about your shop, shug, and that someone was injured. I thought maybe . . ." He took a step back. Looked like he'd bolt any second.

My heart fluttered. Damn. He came to check on me. "Hey, I'm okay. It's Ollie I'm worried about. He's in bad shape."

"The kid who watched the twins the other night?" Tommy stepped closer.

"Yeah, docs are saying he probably won't make it." I kept my voice low so Ollie's parents wouldn't overhear. "They set him on fire."

Tommy's mouth thinned. "You're turning me soft, Poe Dupin."

"What do you mean?"

"Give me a minute." Tommy walked up to the enclosure

and spoke with the stern attendant. A moment later, she buzzed him through, then they both disappeared into the back. I returned to sit next to Ollie's parents.

What was the demon up to now? I never in a million years expected him to turn up here. For me.

"Are you seeing someone, Poe?" Beth asked, swiping at her wet cheeks.

"No. Yes. Maybe?" I tapped my foot, knee bouncing. "I don't really know."

Terry's mouth slightly turned up. "I went through that when Beth and I met."

"Didn't take you long to decide we were dating." She leaned into him.

"No, but it took *you* long enough. I was sweating bullets." He kissed her forehead.

When Tommy shuffled back into the waiting room a few minutes later, dark circles ringed his eyes, and his pink mouth had turned thin and bloodless. His skin had bleached so white he almost glowed, and his golden hair hung sweaty on his brow. He shook as he walked, every step looking more painful than the last.

I shot to my feet. "What—"

"He'll be okay." He raised his voice, then looked at me, his eyes hollow, and a tremor he couldn't hide causing me to reach for him.

"The doctor told you that?" Beth asked, her voice rising with an edge of excitement.

Tommy swallowed. "Heard them talking when I was back there. Doctor should be out momentarily. A miracle."

Liar. He'd done something. But I kept quiet.

"That's wonderful!" Beth and Terry collapsed against one another, resembling marionettes with their strings cut.

Tommy swayed on his feet. I steadied him without being

too obvious. I glanced over my shoulder at Ollie's parents. "Now that we know Ollie's gonna be okay, I'm taking my friend home. It's been a long night. I'll be back first thing in the morning to check on him."

"Thank you, Poe, for all you've done." Beth began to rise from her seat, but her husband, gripped her hand and shook his head.

"I didn't do anything." Tommy did. "But you're welcome."

Before they could respond, I grasped Tommy's elbow and steered him toward the exit. We took the elevator to the ground floor, Tommy's shaking growing progressively worse.

Once outside the hospital, I wrapped my arm around Tommy's waist. He leaned into me, seeming small and frail.

"What did you do?"

"Healed him." Tommy swayed into me more, his steps faltering.

"Where's your ride?"

He nodded to the back lot where his limo was parked. I waved to get the driver's attention.

The limo cruised up with Michael behind the wheel. I opened the back door and herded Tommy inside, then climbed in behind.

The three of us didn't speak as we headed back toward Tommy's territory. We took the neutral routes defined by MASC, so that nobody could accuse us of trespassing. Tommy's breathing sounded labored in the quiet of the car. We cruised into his Neighborhood, past Rumpled Still, and continued down the block to a gleaming high-rise with a light-blue glass exterior.

The limo pulled into the underground parking garage. After going through another gate, we parked in an area that was clearly reserved. I all but lifted Tommy out of the limo. Michael hurried around and reached for him.

Tommy drew back. "Poe has me."

"But Tommy—"

"Goodnight, Michael."

Michael frowned. He reluctantly nodded. "I should at least see you to your place."

Tommy waved him away. "It's okay. Go."

Michael gave me a death glare, warning me with his eyes that I had better take excellent care of Tommy Tittoti. I dipped my chin in acknowledgment. Message received. Nothing would happen to the little demon on my watch.

I helped Tommy toward the private elevator. He placed his hand on the elevator plate. The door slid open, and we entered. He waved to Michael. When the door snapped shut, Tommy collapsed.

17

I swept him into my arms in a bridal carry. His eyes fluttered closed, and he curled up so that his head rested on my shoulder. What. The. Fuck. Should I call Michael back? Or phone a doctor?

The elevator dinged, and the doors slid open. We'd arrived on the top floor, and I stepped directly into Tommy's place. Skylights and an amazing view of the city. Soaring twelve-foot ceilings, a patio ... was that a lap pool?

I should've known.

Rich tapestries hung on the walls, some of them looking ancient. Persian rugs covered marble tile, and comfortable but clearly expensive furniture decorated the living room. A bookshelf with glass doors held heavy, leather bound books. First editions? Was that a Gutenberg Bible?

The hint of apples scented the space.

"Nice place," I commented.

He groaned.

"Sorry." I looked around. Two hallways. I turned right. I guessed correctly. Tommy's bedroom lay at the end of the hall.

Floor-to-ceiling glass windows, and a huge four-poster bed with sheer draping around the sides. "I think you're more fairytale prince than demon."

"Fuck. Off," he wheezed.

I'd have laughed, but just those two words cost him. Pushing past the curtains, I gently placed Tommy on bedding so soft he sunk into it.

He looked so small in the gigantic bed. Did I leave him? I bit my lip.

"Stay." His lashes fluttered, but he didn't open his eyes. He squeezed my wrist.

"'Kay."

He sighed, and his body went limp.

I pulled off his shoes and socks. Should I undress him? His jeans hugged his hips. Couldn't be comfortable. I stripped him out of his shirt, then down to his... *fuuuck* me. Red. Manties. Lacy ones. I about blew my load on the spot. Wasn't he full of surprises? I fingered the lace at his waist before withdrawing my hand like he'd burned me. I'd just leave him in those. I swallowed. I wouldn't be getting that image out of my head anytime soon. I tucked the sheet up around him, so he wouldn't get cold. Uh-huh. Nothing to do with hiding temptation. Nope.

I hurried out of the room. I could sleep on the couch. Or in a guest bedroom. Or should I keep vigil? What if he needed me in the middle of the night?

I rarely shared anyone's bed. Not to sleep in, anyway. But Tommy's weakened state worried me. My gut said stay close, just in case. And if that was a really lame excuse to wrap my body around his for the night, well, I wouldn't question it too closely.

I padded toward the kitchen and rummaged in his walk-in fridge. The entire kitchen was high-end stainless. The refrigerator probably cost more than my shop. He... he had a wine station. Four bottles, glass front for proper display.

Seriously? His built-in espresso machine about made me cream my jeans. At first I didn't even realize it was for coffee. I mean, the thing was huge. And a whole coffee bar that went with it. Coffees that cost several hundred dollars a pound sat in a small coffee fridge on the counter. He even had a wood-fired pizza oven. Holy fuck. Must be nice to live the high life.

I'd choked down a few stale crackers and cheese from the hospital vending machine but otherwise hadn't had anything since morning. I found Indian leftovers. After heating the saag paneer and naan in a microwave that had way too many options, I grabbed a wine glass from over the wine station and randomly pushed a button. It's not like I knew much about wines. The machine dispensed a white. Chilled. Was white supposed to be cold? I shrugged. Good enough.

I ate and considered what to do. Shit, the shock was wearing off. Relief that Ollie would be okay mingled with soul-crushing reality. I'd left Tommy's barber shop feeling elated at the idea of offering members a new roost. Now I had nothing to offer. I was, at least for the moment, as destitute as they were. Damn Briggs. And damn Ethan.

I scrubbed at my face. No time to fall apart. The roost would need my strength. Pushing down the panic, I gulped down my wine, my hand shaking. I'd figure something out. I always did. I needed to remember that.

Once I finished eating, I loaded the dishwasher. The infernal thing beeped at me and an LED readout "suggested" I move the dish to a different part of the loading rack. I snorted but did as it asked.

I then returned to Tommy's room to check on him. Still out.

What had happened? Why was he like this? He'd healed me earlier in the day and didn't have any such reaction.

Didn't help my mood that I was pretty much useless as a nursemaid.

Next, I rummaged in the master bathroom and found a bin full of new toothbrushes. Just how many guests did he have over, anyway? My gut churned with acid. No, I wasn't jealous.

I brushed my teeth with more force than was strictly necessary and glanced in the enormous mirror.

Damn, I was a mess. Didn't even realize I had soot on my clothes and across one cheek. I sniffed. Yeah, I smelled like I'd rolled in a firepit. Only slightly more chemically. I wrinkled my nose. I couldn't sleep like that. I eyed his massive shower. He also had a tub that was big enough for at least four creatures. How many lovers had he... You know what? I didn't want to know. Didn't care. Not me.

Shower it was. I peeled off my clothes, left them in a pile on the floor. He probably had a washing machine, but if it was anything like his kitchen appliances, I'd have no clue how to run it.

I turned the taps to hot and stepped under the multiple nozzles. Jets pelted me, and though tempted to stay in longer and enjoy the luxury, I didn't feel right about it. What if he woke and needed me?

I climbed out, dried off—ooh, heated towel rack, nice—and wrapped myself in a towel. My clothes were a lost cause, and no way Tommy's would fit. I padded back to the bed. Should I?

Why was I making this such a big deal? I didn't obsess over stupid shit.

Fine. I crawled into bed. See, not obsessing.

Tommy looked so small in his huge bed, surrounded by dozens of pillows. Who the hell needed that many pillows?

I lay on my back, trying to keep some distance. As if sensing me, Tommy slid over and snuggled into my side. You wouldn't think a demon would feel so perfect. But he did.

I was so screwed.

18

I woke on my back with Tommy staring down at me. My towel had come off my hips, and I lay naked under his gaze. His eyes glowed red, and his magic crackled around us.

That's what had scared me most last night. His magic hadn't sparked the way I'd grown used to. It had felt like the magic had withdrawn inside. Like a black hole or some shit. But now it surrounded us, and I could all but see tendrils of it.

He smiled, and his fangs lengthened, and claws sprung from his fingertips. "Good morning, shug."

If I had any survival instincts, that should have scared the crap out of me. Instead, I scrubbed at my eyes. "What time is it?"

"Almost 8:30." He ran a gentle claw down my chest, watching the blood well up under the skin.

Blood pooled in other parts of my body, too. I didn't bother to cover up.

"Your magic's back."

"Mmm. Sure is."

"You gonna explain what happened?" I swallowed. He looked like he wanted to eat me up. I'd let him.

He sighed before meeting my gaze. "I can't use my magic without a bargain in place unless it's to defend myself.

When I healed your friend, I hadn't made a deal with him for his health."

I frowned. "But you treated me earlier in the day."

He shifted, broke eye contact. His hand resumed its slow descent down my chest, leaving faint tracks from his claws. "I had a mark coming in. I knew I'd be capturing their . . . magic . . . soon enough. You were too out of it to notice much."

I did remember him saying something about that. Huh. So why did he sit so stiffly now?

"Thank you for saving Ollie. He's a good kid."

He looked up, met my eyes. The red glowed brighter, and for a moment, his magic shimmered. "You're welcome. Thank you for staying."

"I didn't do much. I ate your leftovers."

The corner of his mouth turned up. "You did more than that, shug." He continued his petting.

My cock liked it. A lot. I'd been trying not to look at his manties, but I lost that battle. He was so hot. Something about him being wrapped up in lace and yet so powerful just did it for me.

He smiled. "Like what you see?"

"Oh, yeah." I reached out to run a finger along the lace trim, but he snagged my wrist.

"No, shug. I'm not safe to touch yet." He placed my hand down by my side.

"You gonna blow me up?"

"More like eat you up. Especially if you keep looking at me like that."

"And that's a bad thing?"

He bit his bottom lip, clearly considering something. He kept up a possessive sweep over my chest, and my dick leaked a drop of precome onto my stomach. He swiped a finger through it and brought it to his mouth. Licked it off. He closed his eyes like it was the best thing he'd ever tasted. When he opened his eyes, they glowed a fiery red. "Here's what's going to happen, birdie. You'll lie there and let me do what I want to you. You're not to touch me, understand?"

I raised a brow. Well, hell...

One of his claws pricked my skin, and I jerked, sucked in a startled breath. "Yeah, I get it."

Tommy stood and shimmied out of his manties. He grabbed some lube from the bedside drawer, then climbed back on the bed. He popped the cap and drizzled the cool liquid over my hot skin. He chuckled when I shivered, and he wrapped his hand around my cock. I groaned. So good.

He added more, getting me nice and slick. Rising on his knees, he straddled me.

"Let me prep you first." I lifted a hand toward him, but he caught it once again and slammed it back onto the bed.

"I said no touching, shug. Put your arms above your head and keep them there." He'd left unspoken *or I'll make you.*

I raised my arms. Not a dummy.

He nodded in approval, and it made my insides feel warm.

"You're so damn perfect, birdie."

I would have laughed at the absurd statement, except he chose that moment to slam himself down on my cock. No prep. Just heat and pressure.

I gasped. Oh. Oh, fuck. I had to bite the inside of my cheek to keep this ride from being over too soon.

Tommy didn't go easy on me. He used me like he'd built me just for him, his eyes glowing and so focused on my every expression. Fucking heady stuff. When I unconsciously reached for him, he growled at me—inhuman and downright scary. I loved it.

He rode me fast and hard, his claws digging into my shoulders and sweat dripping from his brow. The sound of our bodies slapping together ramped my lust, made my toes curl.

He tightened around me, and I moaned. Damn, he felt so good. I bucked up. In response, he gripped my hair and slammed our mouths together, his fangs pricking my lip, his tongue commanding me to open for him. I did. He continued his frenzied pace, only letting up when he paused to lick the blood off my lip.

"Mmm, you taste good." He grinned, every bit of it wicked. For a moment, his glide gentled, a slow grinding of the hips as he came down on me. His hand let go of my hair and slid to my neck, putting just enough pressure on my airway so I'd know he *could* hurt me. But he wouldn't.

Another kink I didn't know I had.

I arched. Couldn't help myself. Wanted to go as deep as he'd let me.

He picked up the pace again, letting up slightly on my throat. When he tightened around me, I was a goner.

"Oh, fuck." I threw back my head, my fists clenched so I wouldn't reach for him.

"Look at me, shug. I want to watch you blow. Know I did this to you."

Why was that so hot? I forced myself to keep eye contact as I tipped over the edge, my body rigid. His gaze stayed locked with mine, and he kept the pace rough as I came.

When my body finally went limp, he made a show of retracting his claws and gripped his cock. A few strokes, and he came all over my stomach and chest, marking me. One spurt even hit my chin. He never looked away. When he was totally spent, he ran his palm over my chest, rubbing his come into my skin. I'd never had a lover act possessively toward me before. I liked it. Probably too much to be healthy. But with my brains fucked out, and the smell of apples surrounding me, I just didn't care.

He stayed on my lap watching until I slipped out of him. Then he rolled off the bed and held out a hand. "Come on birdie, let's go clean up."

"I think you broke me." I grinned, my body boneless.

He kept his hand extended. After a moment of hesitation, I grasped it.

"You ain't seen nothing yet, sugar."

19

Mutual blowjobs in the shower meant we stayed in the water until my fingertips pruned and my knees ached from kneeling on the tile. We somehow managed to get clean.

Afterward, Tommy wrinkled his nose at my sad pile of clothes. He dug out my phone and went to toss the clothing in the washer. He pointed to a fluffy robe hanging on the back of the door. I couldn't stay too much longer, almost protested the time it would take to wash and dry everything, but I had questions I needed answers to. So, I donned the robe. Softest thing I'd ever put against my skin. Like being wrapped in a cloud.

When he returned, he handed me a charger for my phone. Shit. My phone. Dead. I plugged it in and turned it on. It blew up with notifications. A ton from Kennedy. Some from Abe. One from Ollie's parents. I texted Kennedy to let her know I was with Tommy. Our text exchange went something like:

Me: Hey.
Her: Dumbass, u better b ok. Saw fire on news.
Me: Fine, thanx 4 asking. I'm @T's.
Her: . . .
Me: Go ahead & say it.

Her: Nope.
Me: *gasps in rich girl *
Her: Screw off. In case u were wondering, I dropped twins @school. UR welcome. If T doesn't let ur sorry ass stay, u can bring kids here.
Me: Only the kids?
Her: I might let u ZZZ on front steps.

That's my bestie.

I also sent messages to Abe and responded to Ollie's parents. Ollie was awake and asking for me. I'd need to see him soon.

When I finished with my messages, I left my phone to charge and followed my nose down the hallway to the kitchen.

Tommy had sausage links sizzling away in a skillet.

"You cook?"

He cocked an eyebrow. "Why so surprised, birdie? When you're slightly over two thousand years old, you pick up a few things."

"Touché. You just seem like the guy who would do a lot of carryout or have a chef cook for you."

"I don't enjoy having too many people in my home and I do a lot of carryout. I like supporting local businesses. But I also enjoy cooking. Especially when I have someone to cook for." He pulled out a pan and began to warm it on another burner.

"I like to cook, too," I offered. "My mom was many things, but she wasn't much of a cook. From the time I was about eleven or twelve, I did all the cooking. Lucy and Jamie love my homemade mac and cheese and my manicotti."

He nodded to the other pan. "Why don't you do the eggs? Over easy, okay?"

I went to work. We cooked side by side.

Tommy stepped up to his monstrosity of a coffee machine and started messing with the levers. A moment later, he handed me a cappuccino.

I inhaled. Moaned.

He snickered. Went to make himself one, while I plated the eggs and sausage.

I took my first sip. Might have qualified for my third orgasm of the morning.

"Fuck, that's good. This must be a $30 cup of coffee." I tried to savor it, but damn, I didn't get coffee like this often. Maybe not ever.

Tommy shrugged. "Little more than that." He took a drink. "Do you know at one time, coffee was cheap. You could get the good stuff for ten or fifteen dollars a pound."

"No way. You're making that up."

"Until the 1980s, coffee was easily available and not the synthetic crap most stores sell today. Real coffee beans." He grinned. "Watching you drink that cup might be better than porn, shug."

I blushed.

Tommy grabbed our plates and set them on a small café table I hadn't even noticed until now. When I finished my cup of coffee, he made me another. We ate in companionable silence.

"Can you ever do something for someone else simply because you want to, or does there have to be a deal in place?" I sort of blurted it out.

Tommy sipped his coffee, considered me. He shrugged. "As long as it doesn't use my magic, I have some leeway. I can offer you breakfast, expecting nothing in return, though my demon nature would always *prefer* a bargain. But that's not realistic in this world, and I don't only want transactional relationships."

Interesting. As a raven shifter, I felt an obligation to my roost. Made sense a demon would have their own nature to contend with. We all had rules and limitations, right?

"Demon got your tongue?" He smirked at me, but something in his eyes looked... hesitant.

"I was thinking about all the different scenarios. If someone you cared about was in danger, could you protect them without a bargain?"

"Depends. I can defend myself. If I'm not under threat, but let's say an innocent bystander was, I could help him at the expense of my magic."

"So you couldn't help Carter, for example, if someone attacked him?"

"I didn't say that. Carter lives in my territory. He's technically... mine. I can defend my people."

"That's why you've claimed this area as your Neighborhood, isn't it? Because if anyone encroaches on your Neighborhood or your people, then it's the same as them attacking you and it gives you a way to defend them."

Tommy's eyes widened slightly. Yeah, I'd surprised him. But it fit.

"Yes, that's true." He tried to sound gruff, but I fucking melted. He protected his people. In my world, that meant everything.

"I'm impressed."

"Don't be." He waved a dismissive hand.

"I am. I assumed you thought of territory the way non-shifter creatures did, but you don't really, do you? Or at least you look at it as a way to keep your people safe."

"Well, it makes little sense to let them get slaughtered. I might need them for things later."

"You know, I don't see caring about people as a flaw. Nor as a weakness. You don't have to pretend they don't matter."

He deflated. "But it *is* a weakness, Poe. When you care, you give people leverage they can use against you. That's why I said you should walk away from your roost. Because as long as you care about them, others will use that against you, shug. Hence your poor little friend in the hospital."

"Yeah, but what's the alternative? Never care about anyone? Seems . . . lonely."

"Lonely, yes. But at least others aren't used to manipulate me."

Not terrible advice. Only he didn't follow it any more than I did. "You do care about others. You may not let them care about you, but the more I think about it, the more obvious it is that they mean something to you. At least enough to put them in your Neighborhood and keep them safe."

Tommy shifted in his chair. I screwed up my nerve.

"Is it hard to kill creatures?" I'd been wanting to know.

"No." He didn't even wince, just took a last sip of his coffee. "Most of the creatures who make deals with me are bad people, Poe. Murderers, rapists with a whole host of other ugliness associated with them. The world is a better place when they're gone."

"What gives you the right to be their executioner?"

He smirked. His amusement genuine this time. "MASC, of course."

I sat up straight. "You can't be serious."

"But I am, sugar. How do you think I got my resident's permit? You think MASC were okay with a demon moving in? The only reason they allow me to stay is because I'm useful. They point people my way."

"So you're really an assassin?" Wow, the rumors had

been right. That should freak me out. Somehow, though, it didn't.

"'Assassin' is such an ugly word, birdie. I like to think of myself as the great leveler. Besides, I give them a chance. That's the deal they make. And they get to figure out whether or not they keep it. But the price for failure is death. Sometimes, they'll fulfill their part of the bargain. Rarely, they'll walk away afterward. I'm always impressed when they do so. Means they probably deserve to live. But most? They bargain again, and again, and again. Until the price becomes too high to meet."

"That seems like a lot of stress."

He laughed, the sound musical and light. Especially for such a dark topic. "I don't think you understand, Poe. Much like vampires need blood to survive, these bargains are part of my nature. They fuel my magic. That's like asking me whether eating is stressful."

"So you keep upping your price until they fail. Eventually, if I ask, I'll fail."

"Yes. But I wouldn't be happy about it in your case. I can't change my nature any more than a vampire can stop drinking blood. I need you to understand that, shug. Societal rules temper my actions, but they don't alter my basic nature."

"Did Carter come to you for a favor?"

He raised a brow. "Yes."

"But he hasn't failed to meet your bargains."

"Bargain. He only asked once. For a cat, he's got a good head on his shoulders."

"You gave him a job. Does he also live in your territory?"

"Yes."

"Did Michael come to you for a deal, too?" Did everyone in his Neighborhood come looking for help?

He narrowed his eyes. "Why so many questions, sugar?"

"Because I don't think you're as terrible as you make yourself out to be. You take care of the evil ones and try to give the rest of us a chance."

He sighed. "I *am* a killer at heart, Poe. You should never forget that."

"I don't want to forget it." I reached over and took Tommy's hand in mine and ran a thumb across the back of his fingers. "I've never killed anyone. But just because you do doesn't scare me. Like you said, you give everyone a chance."

"Then you understand why I don't want you to ask me for the third bargain."

I sighed. "Yeah, I get it. And I like staying alive. There're things I would trade my life for, but I'm not sure that even you could get me what I need. While I can have the buildings rebuilt, we both know that Briggs will only burn them again. So I don't have territory to offer the roost."

"I know. I'm sorry."

"Yeah, me, too."

We sat in silence for a bit. No bargains. Not a hell of a lot of options.

I slumped for a second before forcing my spine straight. "I have a little money saved up, so I'll see if I can rent some apartments. Maybe in the neutral zone if Roger Jones is as pissed off as I think she's gonna be at the ravens for selling out to Briggs. The roost can crash there, unless they want to stay with Briggs. *If* he even provides a place for them."

"Poe, I can offer you a place in my territory." Tommy held up a hand to silence me. "It doesn't come without strings. I can't. I wish I could, but it's not my nature. And I couldn't protect you unless you agree to the terms."

I straightened, narrowed my eyes. "I thought you said not to make a third deal with you."

"This is a little different, because I don't need to use magic to give you what you want."

"What are the terms?"

"You would all be mine. My Neighborhood isn't neutral. Anyone in it belongs to me. That means any businesses you wanted to start, I own. Your roost's homes, I own. You would not have as much freedom to take your extracurricular jobs, because if you mess up, it comes back to my doorstep. You would not have the same freedom you do now."

"So we'd be what exactly? Slaves?"

"No. But I would own *you*. If the rest of your roost gets on their feet and wants to leave, I'd be okay with it. But not you." Tommy looked down at our joined hands, squeezed.

"Why not me?" My voice came out so faint, I could barely hear myself.

He sighed. "Because even though I don't have to use magic, my nature still demands a sacrifice. Your roost would gain safety and over time would prosper. I take care of my people. I would treat you all fairly. But if the roost decided to leave, I still have to have my price met. It would mean you would stay and remain mine." He untwined our hands. "I'm sorry, sugar, it's the best I can do."

"Where would we stay? What would we do? You'd expect us to pay protection, right?" My stomach churned. I'd be a prisoner.

"I don't run my Neighborhood in quite the same way. Unlike the Rogers, I have no need for money. You saw what I'm capable of. Hell, I can even spin straw into gold. And, because of my agreement with MASC, I can't expand my Neighborhood. I have an apartment building where I would put you all up. For those who have outside jobs, they would continue them. For those who need work, I have positions they can fill. Everyone who works in my territory lives in my territory. I don't allow outsiders. The benefit, of course, is that you gain my protection."

"So even if we decided you were unfair, the rest of my roost would be free to go elsewhere? You wouldn't try to stop them or hurt them?"

"I'm a demon, sugar, not a monster."

"How would that work? Would you allow Ethan into your territory?"

"Oh, hell no, birdie. He's out."

"Then how—"

"I'd give *you* the apartments, and they could choose whether to join your roost. If they don't want to, that's fine. If they do, they'll abide by my laws. As will you."

"But let's say we don't like it. Your laws are too strict or whatever. They wouldn't be able to leave without me because I'd now be their alpha. So by owning me, you'd own them."

"Yes, but that depends on their loyalty to you. They could choose to leave and select another alpha. If they were unhappy, I know you would let them go. But you can ask around, my people are satisfied."

"Can I think about it?"

"Sure, sugar. You have my permission to talk to my people, too. When I head to work, I'll drop you by the EA Apartments, and the superintendent will meet you there. Rosine would love to have a building full of tenants. It's only about half capacity now. She can show you the different options available. As the roost alpha, it would be your job to determine where everyone would stay."

"Why are you offering me such a deal? It seems too good to be true."

"For your roost, that's probably true. They get the benefit of your generosity. But your life would change. Because it would never be your own again. That's a pretty steep price for a bird who values his freedom. And that's the kind of bargain that satisfies my nature."

I nodded but didn't look Tommy in the eye. Life in a gilded cage was still a cage.

20

Tommy's offer rolled around in my brain long after he'd gone to work. I stood in the lobby of an ornate brownstone-and-brick high rise. The first three stories were brownstone with pillars framing a twelve-foot round doorway with a bas relief above the entrance that reminded me of some of the oldest churches in Baltimore. A bygone era. Though churches probably didn't use a demon as their theme. The high rise was divided into two towers made from brick with terracotta trim.

The lobby looked like it belonged on an old silent movie set, divans instead of sofas, even a few decorative pillars. The works. Felt as if I should wave around an ivory cigarette holder while discussing my latest safari in Africa. Damn. I couldn't imagine my scraggly ass coming home to such a stately building every night.

Rosine, the superintendent, met me within minutes. A Latinx human, she dressed to the nines in a high-end tailored suit and sky-high heels. Reminded me of Kennedy, except she didn't call me a dumbass even once. She was very enthusiastic and showed several apartment layouts. There were enough spaces for my whole roost. The apartment she said would be mine had three bedrooms and a great view of the city. It also had a balcony. And the complex had a pool and a gym, even a small day care center.

"Rosine, thank you for showing me around." We returned to the lobby, and I couldn't help but be star-struck again. Could this really be home?

But home came at a high price. At least for me. And damn Tommy Tittoti for knowing what would make me bleed.

And yet, I could picture the awe on my roost's faces knowing they'd live in such a space. The twins would love it, too. We could rebuild. If they wanted to leave someday, they could. I wouldn't hold them. I wasn't leadership material, anyway. But with Abe's help, maybe... I stuffed my hands in my pockets, unsure what else to say.

She smiled. "You're wondering whether Tommy's a good guy, huh?"

"Why would you ask that?"

"Because it's a common question when people first come here. He treats us well. And what are the other options? We can move to an unfamiliar territory where we'll be under a harsher reign or we can stay in one of the neutral zones, where everyone has to fend for themselves. Since you have a pack—excuse me, I meant a roost—you might do okay in a neutral zone. But here, you don't have to worry so much. Tommy takes his responsibilities seriously. Anyway, that's my sales pitch. But spend some time walking the Neighborhood and looking in the shops."

"I . . ." She couldn't understand what it felt like to be a low-class bird being given the chance to move into a high-class building. Overwhelming. Uncomfortable. But also a little bit of hope unfurled in my chest. Even though I tried to squash it. Nothing was for free, and opportunities for guys like me were like trying to hold water with my hands.

"You know, I came from Briggs' Bickley's Neighborhood. Used to be a casino girl. I fell into a little trouble with some clientele, and Tommy helped me out. Sent me back to school for hotel and restaurant management." She reached out and squeezed my arm. "You think you're the only one who has washed up on his shores in a desperate situation. But almost everyone here has been in a similar situation. We all know what it's like."

Wow. I didn't know how to handle that. She wore classy as easily as her tailored suit. Couldn't ever see that happening to me. "Thanks again, Rosine. You've given me a lot to think about."

She waved as I exited. Fled, if I'm being honest.

My head was a bit of a mess. I needed time to think. If what she said was true, I could give the twins a better life. And the roost, too. I'd only have to sacrifice myself. And really, I didn't have a lot to contribute, no matter what Rosine said.

When I crossed back over into Raven territory, or what had been our territory, the street was a disaster. Ashy, sooty, and waterlogged. I'd need to deal with insurance and other issues. I also needed to run by the hospital and see Ollie. But Abe had been blowing up my phone for the last hour. One crisis at a time.

I rounded the corner and stopped in my tracks. Machinery everywhere. Two—no, three—cranes with wrecking balls, several dump trucks, bulldozers, and lots of SUVs with Briggs' snakehead logo. What. The. Fuck.

Briggs had to have sent every enforcer he had. They seemed to delight in waving their firepower around at the terrified ravens. Ravens, their arms full of household possessions, cried as they sat in a circle in the road surrounded by Briggs' small army. Other enforcers tossed bits and pieces of people's lives out onto the street. Laughing when precious items smashed on the pavement.

Scanning the crowd, I found Andre—that pig fucker—right in the middle of the chaos with a goddamned smile on his too smug snout. He leaned against one of the cranes.

A muscle in my jaw ticked. I strode in his direction, and when a bear shifter stepped into my path I throat-punched him without a second thought. He dropped like a stone. These larger shifters thought they were invincible. Stupid fucks. I kept walking, beelining toward Andre. Other shifters stepped into my way, but Andre called them off. Yeah, it was on.

He grinned as I stomped up to him, took a swing. You'd think he would have expected it. I snapped his head back, broke his snout. As he groaned and moved to cover his face from another blow, I kicked him as hard as I could right in the nads. Guy never learned.

He doubled over.

Sure, I found myself surrounded, more guns than I had fingers pointed at my head. Maybe not my smartest move. I'd also broken a few knuckles. Worth it.

Andre managed to pull himself upright. Boar shifters were tough, I'd give them that.

"You're dead." He took a step toward me.

Shit. Maybe I should have thought this out a little better.

"You don't want to touch me. Tommy wouldn't like that."

Andre froze in his tracks.

Huh. Hadn't expected that. Kind of thought he'd laugh and just kick my ass. Sensing weakness, I smirked. "Yeah, hurting his little fuck toy won't endear you to him. And since I belong to him, I'm pretty sure he'd eat your soul for a snack. But, I mean, sure, go ahead, take a swing, asshole."

Andre's fists clenched and unclenched. "Put him with the others. He can watch as we clear the way for progress."

If he said "visionary," I might throw up. "You can't legally tear these down. Ethan only signed them over yesterday. There'd have to be at least a 30-day notice."

Andre shrugged. "Go ahead and try to get an injunction. I hear it takes 24 hours. We'll be done by that time."

"No way Roger Jones would be okay—"

"Hear she's having some trouble on the north side of her Neighborhood today. She's pretty busy. Unrest is a bitch." He wiped the blood from his face with his sleeve. He nodded toward one shifter. The hard, cold barrel of a gun pressed into my back. "Put him with the others."

I didn't resist. My mind whirred a hundred miles an hour. How did I stop this? Could I stop this?

I stepped into the circle of ravens, and they all called to me like they were drowning and I was in the only lifeboat. Maybe I was. Abe limped over to me, his arm hanging at a weird angle. Dislocated shoulder. I'd had that one many times, thanks to Ethan.

"Man, why didn't you have someone help you?" I sniped. Before he could say anything, I stepped into him, grasped his arm, and popped his shoulder back into its socket.

He howled.

Hated to do it, but better taken by surprise than waiting for it to happen. Learned that the hard way, too.

"Damn, Poe. Warn a guy." Abe rubbed at his bicep.

"Trust me, I did you a favor. How's it feel now?"

"Like you tore my arm off and reattached it."

"So, better, then."

Abe snorted.

"Why didn't you tell me this shit was going on, Abe? You sent me a hundred damned texts this morning. Think you could have mentioned the wrecking crew."

"They showed up, took our phones." His locs fell into his

face as he glared at the guards from under his lashes. "What are we going to do?"

Do? Wish I knew. But that's not what he wanted to hear.

"Where's Ethan?" I asked.

"Haven't seen him." Abe bared his teeth.

I raked a hand through my hair. "He's supposed to have housing for us."

"News to me." Abe rubbed at his arm again.

Well, fuck.

My phone buzzed in my pocket. Fortunately, I had the ringer off, so it didn't draw the guards' attention. Abe and a few of the others crowded around. I pulled the phone out and looked at the number. Tommy Tittoti's name lit up my screen. What the hell? When did he have time to enter his name into my contacts?

"Hello?" I kept my voice as quiet as possible.

"You okay, birdie?" Tommy's voice came out clipped.

"I mean, yeah, if being surrounded by a shitload of Briggs' guys at gunpoint is considered okay, then I'm great."

Tommy cursed under his breath.

"How d'you know I'd be in trouble?"

A pause.

"Shug, you are the definition of trouble. What do you need?"

"If I take you up on your offer, how soon would we be able to move in?"

The line went so quiet that I thought we'd been disconnected.

"Hello? Tommy?"

"Are you sure you want to do this, Poe?"

"No. But I don't see a lot of other options. Briggs' goons are tossing everyone and their stuff onto the street as we speak. No one has a place to go. They've got wrecking equipment and everything."

"Dammit. That's why Jos is tied up with riots. Briggs is sneaky, I'll give him that." Tommy sighed. "In a half hour, Carter will be there. He'll tell you what to do. If I could give you your freedom, I would. I'm sorry, Poe."

"Yeah, me too."

∽

TOMMY WAS a demon of his word. Carter arrived before the half hour was up. Only it wasn't just Carter but a caravan of moving trucks. Damn, Tommy didn't mess around. The ravens cheered when they saw the trucks, and Andre gaped. The drivers were all shifters of one sort or another, and Carter rode shotgun in the lead truck. His pink hair and bubblegum pink lip gloss stood out like a beacon as he disembarked. Naturally, he chomped obnoxiously on a piece of gum. That cat had a hardcore oral fixation.

He came straight to us, an extra swing to his slim hips. Briggs' enforcers parted without even attempting to block him.

"Hey, rockstar, heard you guys needed a hand?" He looped his arm through mine in way of greeting and tugged me toward the trucks. The guards didn't move aside this time. He tilted his head. "You sure you want to go this route?" He batted his lashes, smacked his gum.

They exchanged looks and slowly stepped away.

"Thanks, boys." He winked at them.

Cheeky cat. Hated to admit it, but I kind of liked the guy.

We ambled to the back of his truck. Andre strode toward us, his expression thunderous. His nose had a distinct kink to it now, and he'd stuffed tissue into his nostrils to stem the bleeding.

"Ooh, please tell me you did that to him, rockstar."

"I did."

"Knew I liked you." He petted me absently while watching Andre approach.

"You can't park here, cat. This is Briggs Bickley's territory. You're trespassing."

"Awww, I didn't realize pig shifters were so slow. This is Josephine Jones' Neighborhood last time I checked. Regardless of what your snaky overlord thinks."

"Watch it, pussy. Accidents happen." He cracked his knuckles like he was in some bad gangster movie.

"Yeah, they do." Carter continued chewing his gum. Even blew a bubble. "But I think you got that backwards, piggy. Pretty sure you're the one who's leaving." He lifted the lever on the back of the truck, and the door shot up. Creatures of all types filed from the back. Mages, shifters, vampires, even a human or two. There had to be 50 or more of them. "Let's get to it, y'all."

Andre goggled. "You can't—"

"Think we established that I can. Got a problem with it? Take it up with Tommy Tittoti." Carter pulled a business card from his pocket and flicked it at Andre. Considering a glowing mage stood behind Carter, her hair billowing around her head and lightning crackling in her palms, Andre snatched the card and stormed off to safer ground.

"Should have brought weapons, and not only a couple of low-level sorcerers," Andre called. He made some angry hand signals to his crew, and they turned their guns on the captive ravens. Oh, shit.

Carter snorted. "Damn, stupid grows on trees around here." He reached in his pocket and pulled out a small chess piece that he held between his thumb and forefinger. A knight? "Stand back, rockstar."

He tossed the knight as far away from the trucks as he could.

Guns tore from the arms of Briggs' army, sometimes breaking arms and fingers as the weapons shot toward the chess piece and disappeared into it. Not a single weapon remained.

I gaped.

"Pretty impressive, huh? Tommy has lots of fun little surprises." Carter grinned, his lip gloss sparkling in the sunlight.

Andre and his crew stood stock still. Carter gave Andre a one-finger salute. "Suggest you all run along now. Not so tough without your weapons, are you?"

A couple of vampires—garbed all in black and wearing wide-brimmed hats with black funeral netting—moved to the fore and bared their fangs.

"Ooh, they look hungry, don't they, Poe?" Carter quipped.

"Starved. I bet pig tastes real good."

Amazing how quickly Briggs' army could retreat. Seemed they were getting lots of practice recently. I shouldn't feel so smug since I had little to do with it. But I did, anyway. I'll take the victories where I can.

Within a surprisingly short time, we'd loaded everyone's possessions onto the trucks. I had to leave in the middle of it to pick up the twins from school. I didn't want them walking back into this mess unprepared. Fortunately, Kennedy, in her wisdom, had already broken the news about my shop, and they were wearing new outfits that she'd provided. I secretly think she kept a closet just for them, because she provided a good portion of their wardrobe. Lucy and Jamie had asked a million questions, but once we turned onto our street, they jumped into helping families haul their stuff to the trucks.

Then we were on our way. Most of the ravens shifted and took to the air, but we loaded the kids too young to shift into the cabs of the trucks and headed toward our new home.

My whole body trembled. I hoped I hadn't made a huge mistake.

21

The roost loitered in the lobby of the Edgar Allan complex, Rosine walking among them with a tablet. On my initial visit, I hadn't realized that was the full name since Rosine had referred to it as EA Apartments. Figured. Some sort of poetic shit to be found in that, but no time to dwell.

"Listen up, everyone!" When the roost continued to talk, I put my fingers in my mouth and whistled. That worked. All eyes turned my way.

"Tommy Tittoti has granted me some apartments." My face heated. Just saying it sounded like I was the fuck toy I'd pretended to be with Andre. No help for it. And maybe I was. Something to think on . . . later. "This is now *my* territory. Anyone who'd like to join my roost is welcome here. I'll provide a comfortable living space, but in exchange, I will be the roost's alpha. If you're uncomfortable with this arrangement and would like to stay with your current roost, I understand and wish you well. I can have the trucks drop you off at a hotel or somewhere else in the city. Ethan is supposed to have housing for you all."

Abe snorted.

Yeah, the key phrase, "supposed to." Slimy fucker. Still, I wouldn't keep anyone against their will. If they didn't want to accept me, well, my hands were tied.

I waited for someone to challenge my right to be leader. *I'd* sure as shit challenge my right if I were a roost member.

"I know this isn't the usual way of doing things. You're all free to leave at any time to seek another alpha in a different territory if you feel that I'm unfit for the position. I won't hold you here." It needed to be said. They'd already had so many choices stripped from them, and I'd give them the freedom I'd never have again.

"I accept your offer gladly, Alpha." Abe stepped forward and placed his hands together in front of his heart. His hands glowed an inky black, and his bond settled in my chest like a fishhook. Whoa. I staggered from the unexpectedness of it all.

Several others came forward and accepted, their bonds twinning around my heart. Their strength filled me with wonder. How could Ethan not appreciate the gift they'd given him? I wasn't a crier, but the raw emotion filling me with each raven's acceptance brought a suspicious wetness to my eyes. I blinked to hold it at bay. I needed to show the roost I could be a strong alpha. A fair one. Someone who would take care of them all.

In the end, every raven and their families accepted my offer. That only left the twins. I couldn't bind them to me. Only Ethan could do that. Not that he ever would. Both kids gripped my hands, their eyes brimming with tears when they'd tried unsuccessfully to join my roost. I crouched down to their level.

Lucy's lip trembled, and for once, Jamie comforted her.

"It doesn't matter. You're both mine. I'll never give you back. I promise. And when you're old enough, you can make your own decision. We're more than a roost. We're family."

They threw themselves into my arms. We held each other, the three of us. I'd protect them with my life.

Lucy finally leaned back from our embrace, swiped at her tears. "You're being awfully lazy for an alpha."

Jamie sniggered. "Yeah, I want to see my room."

When I looked around, Rosine had things well in hand. She'd separated everyone into family groups. She smiled and made her way over with a tablet. "I have some suggestions for specific spaces for some families' needs, Alpha Dupin. If you have a moment, we can settle these arrangements and then get them unloaded. I understand the trucks are backing up traffic."

And that's how I became a roost alpha.

～

That evening, pizza "mysteriously" arrived for the roost at my apartment, and after we ate together, I sent everyone off to their new homes. They needed to get unpacked and settled. Abe stuck around until I kicked him out. As much as I liked the guy, I didn't need him mother-henning me.

Lucy and Jamie were in their bedrooms oohing and aahing at the new furniture and toys. I'd been pretty shocked to walk in and find the place fully furnished when only this morning it sat empty. Not just furnished, but fit for a rockstar. I didn't know much about decorating, but none of the pieces matched, and yet it looked like it was supposed to be that way.

The living room alone held two leather sofas, one brown, the other gray with a brown stripe, and two gray chairs in clashing styles. Made for plenty of sitting room. An overstuffed chair that looked suspiciously like the one in Tommy's break room sat in a corner next to a floor lamp in the shape of a dragon. Several blue rugs in different shades, two huge round hanging light fixtures that looked like they belonged in a castle, iron rod bookcases, and some framed black and white Billie Holiday prints completed the look. And the rest of the place held more of the same. I'd never even owned a new piece of furniture, so having all this was both cool and unnerving.

After everyone had cleared out, I sank into the overstuffed chair. My arms and back ached from all the lifting. But I wasn't gonna be the kind of alpha to let others work while I sat on my ass. I might not be a natural-born leader, but I'd had enough time around Ethan to know what poor leadership looked like. I'd just do the opposite.

I settled myself deeper in the chair, the smell of apples faint, but distinct. Ugh. I needed no more reminders of Tommy. Especially now that I wasn't sure exactly what we were. Was I his pet? Fuck toy? Enforcer? I couldn't refuse him anything. Not if I wanted to keep my roost safe—or stay alive. But would he demand that I come to his bed? Unlikely. And if he didn't, would I be okay with that? I wasn't the sharpest beak in the flock, but I knew I liked the guy. Like, a lot. Only since I'd accepted his offer, *we* couldn't be a *we*. That's not how these things went.

I ran a hand through my hair. I needed a shower and a good night's sleep. Plenty of time to think about all this in the coming days.

At the quiet knock at my door, I groaned.

No. More. People.

I loved my roost, but I craved some downtime. Should I ignore it? Nah. Being the alpha, I now had responsibilities.

Sighing, I heaved myself from the chair. I trudged to the door, my muscles screaming in protest, and grudgingly opened it, pasting on a smile.

Tommy stood in the doorway wearing his Converse, skinny jeans, and hoodie combo, with the handles of two enormous shopping bags from a high-end department store slung across his wrists. He held them up. "Thought I'd better check on you, sugar, to make sure you have everything you need. These are from Kennedy. She said you'd all need some clothing."

"Oh, yeah, thanks. We're good." I didn't fidget but came close. I took the clothes from him and waved him inside. Placing the bags on the living room floor, I offered him a seat on my brand new sofa. "Everyone's thrilled with their accommodations, and no one seemed to bat an eye with me being the alpha. Guess you were right."

His mouth pulled up at one corner, but he didn't sit. "Yeah, shug, that's not surprising."

"That they accepted me? Or that you were right?"

His grin went full wattage. "You'll have to guess."

His smile made my heart skip a beat. Then it thumped heavy in my chest. This couldn't work. Whatever *this* was. He owned me now, the way Briggs had wanted to. He might not be a cruel master, but he was still a master. My master.

At the same time, it wasn't fair to hold it against him. He'd been honest about his nature from the beginning. He didn't trick me. And I'd accepted what he offered.

We stood there, the quiet stretching between us.

He looked everywhere but at me. "Okay then, I'll let you get settled in, birdie. Why don't you stop by the shop in a couple of days and give me your list of people who need employment, along with their skills. If you have other concerns, we can talk then. Call Carter, and he'll schedule you in." He sounded like he was talking to a stranger.

So, *that's* how it was gonna be? Probably for the best. Still, he'd saved us all. "I . . . thank you. Thank you for what you've done. You've made my roost so happy."

He sighed, stuffed his hands in his hoodie pockets. He

gazed at his feet, and a lock of hair fell onto his forehead. Made him look so young and innocent. "But not you."

What did I say to that?

"I—"

"Listen, Poe . . ." He shook his head, peeked at me from under long blond lashes. "Have a good night, sugar. Give Carter a call."

He turned and walked out, shutting the door quietly behind him. The click of the lock was like the closing of our chapter. A pretty damn brief chapter. But intense. I'd never felt . . . or hoped before.

Maybe we had more to say to each other. Maybe not. Either way, I needed some time to sort it all. I'd call Carter in a couple days, like Tommy said. Maybe I'd have some clarity then.

22

I didn't call Carter. It had only been ten days, and the roost was still settling in. The kids were in a new school, and while they seemed to like it, they were also sad to leave their friends. Not having Ethan in our lives was a blessing, but it meant I needed to be the full-time parent now. I made all the decisions, dried all the tears, and tried my best to be both mom and dad. Not an unfamiliar role, but with the added responsibilities of roost alpha and our new living situation, I got little time to myself or to think about anything not kid or roost related.

Shit, I'd gotten good at lying to myself. Okay, I thought of Tommy all the fucking time. Small moments. Quiet moments. Late-night moments. I'd all but convinced myself this was for the best. Just sex. One and done. Or several and done. Whatever.

Besides, it's not like he texted me. Or stopped by. Or . . . even seemed all that interested.

Once I'd gotten as far as the outside of Rumpled Still, but when I'd looked through the plate-glass window, he'd been laughing with a client, a guy who'd been awfully handsy. I'd have broken some fingers if a dirtbag touched me like that. But not Tommy. Seemed to like the attention. So, yeah, I turned back around and left.

Decision made. Book closed.

This evening, I sat in the living room with Abe and a few other roost members, compiling the list Tommy had asked for. About a third of the roost, whose skills ranged from welding to baking, needed jobs. I'd ask Abe to drop it off for me. You know, because an alpha kept busy. Not because I was a coward or anything.

Ollie curled up in the comfortable chair, trying to look unassuming. We'd sheared his hair close, and he still had a few bandages on his arms and one on his lower back that I helped him change daily. With Tommy's healing, he wouldn't even scar. At least not physically.

I wanted to train Ollie as my assistant. He needed a job but wasn't functional yet. Since the fire, he'd been even more skittish around others. Couldn't blame him. From what little he told me, Briggs' crew hadn't been merciful. Fuckers.

Abe was a great beta and helped me navigate roost dynamics. But I needed someone to keep notes for me and give me reminders. I couldn't remember all the little things I had to do every day.

"Poe, I beat Lucy at chess!" Jamie crowed from his bedroom.

"Only because you cheated." Lucy stomped into the living room, glared at all of us. She pointed at me. "Tell him he's not allowed to cheat."

They'd been squabbling like this the last few days. Ollie hopped up, looked down his nose at Lucy. About as fierce as a hatchling.

"You cheat all the time, Luce."

She sucked in an indignant breath, before breaking out in a huge grin. "That's only with you, Ollie. And you let me get away with it."

Ollie's ears turned bright red. "Well, maybe Jamie thought he could get away with it, too, since you do it."

She narrowed her eyes. "Come play."

Could swear I heard her mutter, "It's not like Poe has time for us." The guilt was coming from all quarters.

"Oh, I'm—" Ollie began, looking my way.

"It's okay, Ollie. I'm good." Wasn't too hard to see he'd rather be with the twins than here, anyway. He gave me a grateful look and let her drag him away. I'd have to spend some time with the kids tonight. Lucy wasn't wrong. I missed them, too.

My phone lit up with a text. I expected it to be Kennedy, but it was from Tommy. My heart leapt into my throat.

"What is it, Alpha?" Abe asked, looking up from his tablet.

I still hadn't gotten used to the title.

"Huh? Oh, nothing." I hesitated before I opened it.

Tommy: Jos asked for a commission. It's going down tomorrow afternoon at MASC HQ. I'll be attending. Need you and Ollie to come with me.
Me: Why us?
Tommy: Because you'll both press a claim against Briggs for the fires. MASC is your best shot at redress.
Me: Ollie isn't in any shape to do that.
Tommy: I'm not asking. See you tomorrow at 3. Be ready. T.

Well, if that didn't say I didn't mean shit to him, I don't know what did. Asshole. I jammed my phone back into my pocket like it had done me wrong. Didn't know how I'd break it to Ollie.

OLLIE HADN'T TAKEN the news well. I'd offered to let him stay at my place tonight, but he'd worried he'd scare the kids with the ramblings and screams from his nightmares. Poor guy. Couldn't catch a break. I wanted to give him his own apartment, but at least for now, he'd be staying with his parents. They were doing a bang up job making up for their lack of attention before the fire.

The others—Abe included—had returned home to their families. I'd spent some time telling the twins funny fairytales my dad had made up when I was a kid, before tucking them into bed. I'd thrown on a new butter-soft pair of flannel pajama bottoms but hadn't bothered with a shirt. The apartment was plenty warm, I just liked the feel of the pants.

I'd only just sunk into my favorite armchair when a crisp knock sounded at the door. A *rat-tat-tat*. Kennedy. She'd stopped by a couple times since we'd moved in. Mostly to drop off more clothing and spoil the kids. For being such a hardass, she had a real soft spot for kids. Or at least the twins.

Striding to the door, I opened it, and raised a brow. She wore a skintight pair of black leather pants, matching leather bustier, and pointy-toed heels that could double as shivs in a pinch.

"Damn, is it dominatrix night at one of the clubs?"

She pushed past me, ignoring the quip. Huh. Not like her. She stomped into the living room, spun around, then pointed to the couch. "Sit."

Okaaay. I inched toward the couch as her hands moved to her hips. "What did I do?"

"You really don't fucking know, do you?" She growled from deep in her chest. Girl would make a wolf shifter proud.

Shit, this was serious. Kennedy didn't swear hardly ever. Well, I mean, if you didn't count "dumbass." What *had* I done? I scratched my head, thinking back over the week. Her birthday wasn't for a couple months yet . . .

"Don't hurt yourself. It'll come to you." She pursed her lips, pointed toward the couch again.

I held my hands up in a pacifying gesture. "Chill. I'm sitting."

I sat, crossed my arms. I couldn't think of one thing—

"Why are you fucking this up?" she asked.

Whoa. The f-bomb twice in one conversation. I blinked. Wait, what? "Fucking what up?"

"You and Tommy." She stomped her foot. Good thing she stood on a rug or she would have left a divot in the wood floor.

"There is no me and Tommy."

"You are such a dumbass. I love you, but I didn't go through all this trouble to match-make, only to have you screw it up with some self-defeatist—" she waved her hand at me, "—whatever this is."

I gaped. Uh, what now? "I'm not—"

"Listen, hon, you know I don't love you for your brains, or your sparkling personality, or your gothy-hobo-chic fashion sense . . . where was I going with this?" She tapped her chin with a nail that she'd filed to a point. "Oh, right. You're my best friend, and I want to see you happy. Tommy Tittoti can make you very, very happy."

I huffed. "Why are we talking about—"

"He's crazy about you. I've never seen him like this about anyone ever. The fact he hasn't tossed you over his shoulder and carried you off to his cave—"

"Penthouse—"

"Whatever, work with me on the imagery—is a wonder."

"Kens, I appreciate you coming over to fuck with my head. What are best friends for, amirite? But I'm a convenience at best. And what makes you think I would—"

"Spare me. We know you'd be shacked up and playing house if you weren't so *you*. Hell, you'd have his ass babies if you could."

Uh . . . wow, imagery I didn't need. "Not sure how to answer that."

"Did you sleep with him?"

"I'm not dead. And you know I did."

"More than once?" She paced in front of the couch but didn't sit.

I shrugged. "Sure. I'm a good lay, he's a demon."

"Tommy doesn't do repeats."

"Well, I don't usually, either, but we're . . . compatible in bed." Really, really compatible.

"Uh-huh. He ever blow you and not expect you to return the favor?"

"That's a little personal . . ." But he had. At his shop that day.

"I knew it! Damn, he's even more gone than I imagined. Giving you freebies. You should be proud. Not everyone struts in and snags a two-thousand-year-old demon." Kennedy gave me the smuggest smile.

I pinched the bridge of my nose. "Look, I haven't snagged anyone. Why would he want to be with me? It's one thing for me to warm his bed. But trust me, he doesn't have feelings for me." I clicked on the text message he'd sent and handed her my phone so she could see for herself.

She whistled. "Man, he's got it bad. When this all works out, he is so going to owe me."

"Where in that message did you get 'he's got it bad for Poe?'"

"What gives, hon? Why aren't you making a move on the guy? I *know* you. You like him. Maybe you even *lurve* him." Kennedy sank down next to me, placed her hand on my knee. "Why won't you let yourself be happy?"

I stared at the floor. "I'm not trying to make myself miserable, I swear. Okay, maybe I like the guy. A little." Or a lot.

She snorted.

I scratched my cheek, making sure I flipped her off while doing it, but still couldn't meet her eyes. "Doesn't matter what I feel. We can't work."

"Why not?" Her hand squeezed my knee. Tight. Painfully so.

I met her gaze. "I'm his *property*, Kens." I winced. "That's the deal I made. Don't you get it? He made me give up the one thing I had that was my own."

"Your ass?" She squinted at me. "You give that out all over the place, anyway."

"No! My *freedom*. That was the bargain. I belong to him now."

Her mouth rounded in an 'o'. Then she laughed. Not a chuckle. A full on belly laugh. What the hell?

"I'm glad you think this is so funny," I spat, made to rise, but she gripped my forearm in a steel grip.

She wiped a tear from the corner of her eye. "Oh, hon, I'm sorry. I'm not laughing at . . . well, yeah, actually I am." She took a deep breath. "Real talk. You are the least free bird I know."

"I—"

"Don't interrupt. It's rude. You've acted as the twins' parent since your mom died. You take care of the roost. Now you're the alpha, which you should have been all along. You owned and ran the community center, with funds you stole from rich assholes, to make sure people had a place to go and to keep young ravens out of trouble. You took in Ollie. Hell, you even let me in, and we know what a terrible decision that was." She squeezed my forearm. "You've never been free, sweetie."

My cheeks burned. She made good points, but Tommy was different. "I might as well be his whore. If he snapped his fingers, I'd *have* to be in his bed. Before, I always made the choice. I *chose* my bed partners, I *chose* to take care of the twins, and Ollie, and even your sorry ass."

"So choose him, too."

"What do you mean? I can't just choose *him*."

"God, you're so melodramatic. Why the hell not? You think you're trapped? Ha! Try being a two-thousand-year-old demon who's crazy about a mangy raven shifter. He didn't have to offer you refuge. When he stood up to Briggs Bickley for you, he knew he'd have to take you in and anyone you cared about. He did it, anyway."

"Yeah, okay, but—"

"He's given you a safe place to live, a chance for your roost to prosper, and has he even once expected you to fawn over him or hang off his arm like a fine piece of ass? Seriously, how do you not pay attention to these things? If you're trapped, *so is he*." Kennedy slapped my thigh. "And even worse, he's put you nearby so he can torture himself by seeing you, yet not make any moves on you . . . because he knows you value your *freedom*—" she made air quotes, "—and he's doing his best to give you what he can. Because he cares."

My eyes widened. Was that what he was doing? "He's . . . why doesn't he say it?"

"Why don't you?"

"Because I don't have any of the power in this relationship!" I yanked at my hair.

"So you admit it's a relationship." Kennedy smirked.

"Ha ha."

"I'm serious, hon. You have a lot more power than you realize." She sighed and rested her head on my shoulder. "You've never been treated as you deserve. It's given you a warped perspective on who you are and what you have to offer. Tommy's not stupid. He sees you. Probably better than anyone."

In some ways, that's exactly what I was afraid of.

23

I walked the twins to school the next day. Ollie's dad agreed to collect them from school and keep them until Ollie and I returned from our meeting with the MASC. It upset both Beth and Terry that Ollie would need to face Briggs. I wasn't happy about it, either, but Tommy hadn't given us a choice.

I'd dressed in my usual all black with a faded vintage Frank Zappa concert tee that had to have cost Kennedy a pretty penny. Tommy hadn't ordered me to wear anything in particular, and it's not like I had much in the way of dress clothes, anyway.

Tommy had sent me another text saying he'd be by around 1 p.m. to pick us up. In the meantime, I called to check on the status of my insurance claim—pending—then took care of roost business until noon. I choked down a pit beef sandwich with extra horseradish and a bag of Utz that one of the roost had left behind last night. As much as I craved a little liquid courage, I didn't want to face Briggs impaired.

Ollie and I still had ten minutes to meet Tommy in the lobby. My stomach knotted. Could Kennedy be right? Seemed . . . unlikely. But I'd never known her to be wrong. Not that I'd tell her that. She had a big enough ego.

A knock at the door had me calling, "Come on in, Ollie, it's open." I knelt to lace up my boots.

"Shouldn't keep your door unlocked, shug. You never know who may show up."

Hair rose on the back of my neck, and goosebumps raced down my arms. I took a calming breath. The tempting smell of apples made that impossible. I shuddered. And not in revulsion. Fuck, seeing Tommy was a bad idea.

I finished tying my laces before looking up and giving him my best shit-eating grin. "I like living on the edge."

He raised a brow. Tommy wore another bespoke suit, a black wool one that fit his slim build to perfection. His hair didn't have a strand out of place. His magic crackled around him, making him seem bigger. Powerful.

We stared at each other. Before I could think better of it, I stood and crowded him against the door. His eyes widened in surprise. I slammed my mouth down on his. Not the smoothest move, but I wasn't a words guy. I liked action. If I ended up skewered on the end of his claws, I guess I'd have my answer.

He gasped against my mouth, and I swept my tongue over his lower lip, asking for entrance. Instead, he pulled back, his hand clasping my throat in an iron grip. His eyes glowed red, and as I watched, his fangs dropped.

Shit. I'd gone too far. In for a penny . . . I pushed further into his grip, constricting my own breath. He instantly eased the pressure.

"Oh, sugar, you should *not* have done that."

One minute I'd had him pinned to the door, the next we'd switched places, the back of my head slamming against the wood. He released my neck.

I gulped in air.

"No, shug, you take your breath from me." He fused our

mouths together, stealing what little air I had. Oh, fuck, his mouth wasn't gentle, his fangs piercing my bottom lip and tongue demanding entrance to my mouth. I gladly gave it to him.

His erection pressed against my thigh, and mine strained against my jeans. I'd missed his taste. The apple flavor made me dizzy with its intensity.

Now this is what I'm talking about.

I arched against him, and a moan so fucking filthy rumbled from my abused throat. If all the blood hadn't gone to my dick, I'd die from embarrassment. Fuck, it was almost a whimper. I had it bad.

He stepped back, released me.

What? No! I reached for him but found myself spun around and forced roughly into the door, my cheek against the wood, Tommy's hand pressing between my shoulder blades. His other hand moved to my fly.

"You're playing with fire, birdie." Tommy's voice had dropped a full octave and sounded more animal than human.

I panted against the door, pushing my ass back asking for more.

He'd gotten my jeans unzipped and unbuttoned and had just wrapped his hand around my leaking cock when someone knocked at the door. We both froze. No.

Another knock.

Fuuuck.

Tommy released me. I could hear his harsh breathing. When I turned, he glowed red, his magic spinning around him like a mini tornado. Holy fuck.

"Answer that, shug." He sprinted down the hall. The bathroom door slammed.

"Poe?" Ollie called through the door. "Is everything okay?"

I groaned and leaned against the door as I tucked myself away. I was gonna have one wicked case of blue balls.

"Hold on, Ollie. Be right there."

Fuckity, fuck, fuck.

~

OLLIE CROWDED me in Tommy's limo, all but sitting on my lap. Each mile closer to MASC HQ, he paled a little more. At this rate, he'd pass out before we ever entered Fort McHenry. I threw an arm around his shoulders, as he burrowed into my side. I glared at Tommy. Why did Ollie need to go through this? I'd face Briggs gladly, but Ollie wasn't strong enough.

Tommy didn't flinch. Damn him. His face remained blank, but he didn't fool me. His magic still swirled dangerously, snapping and crackling. Weird thing, Ollie didn't seem to notice. Nor did Michael. Or if they did, they didn't say anything.

I sank into the luxurious upholstery, trying not to think about what Tommy and I'd done previously in the back of the car. The damn smell of apples in such a tight space didn't help, either. Ugh, I already had a half-chub. Only Ollie's fear kept me from going fully hard.

As we cruised down Key Highway, Tommy and I sat as far away from each other as possible without being obvious. Still felt like we were way too close. Minutes ticked by, and we turned onto East Fort Avenue. We passed the Domino Sugar sign. Not lit up quite yet. I couldn't help but smile when I saw it. Reminded me of the time when I was a little younger than the twins and my dad had brought me to Fort McHenry. We'd had a great day together, picnicking and exploring. I'd had no idea the direction my life would take. Just a dumb, carefree kid.

"Earth to birdie. Did you hear what I said?" Tommy leaned back in his seat, his legs crossed, looking calm and so in control.

"Nope."

"You need to follow my lead. We'll be meeting MASC's Baltimore representative. Garrett Raggnarsson is . . . interesting."

"Is that your way of saying dangerous? Or asshole? Or both?"

Tommy's lips twitched. "Oh, he's dangerous. And can be an asshole. But he's also fair. Don't cross him and you've nothing to fear." His gaze lingered on mine for an extra moment. Warning?

I don't *try* to piss off powerful creatures. I just seemed to have a knack for it. We all had our talents, right?

"Also, make sure you don't look Briggs in the face." He pulled out the necklace he'd loaned Lucy from his suit collar. "If you don't think you can do that, I'll give you the necklace, but I'm planning to keep him solely focused on me."

"I can avoid eye contact." I didn't want Tommy unprotected. In a room full of predators, I was a gnat. Briggs might swat me, but I'd be an afterthought.

We continued into Locust Point, the harborside area where Fort McHenry sat. The areas outside the fort had at one time been seafood restaurants, taverns, and sports bars. Families would eat and then go spend the day at the fort. In the last few years, Briggs had torn the restaurants down in favor of strip clubs and massage parlors.

Tommy frowned, rubbed his chin, as we passed yet

another strip club. "Garrett can't be happy about this. It must affect tourism at the fort."

That's what he's thinking about at a time like this?

Once we'd turned on Constellation Drive, Ollie began to gasp, his breath erratic.

"I can't do this." He gripped my jacket. "I-I can't. I'm not brave like you."

"Hey, it's all right—"

"Ollie." Tommy's voice remained calm, but it radiated strength.

Ollie's head snapped up, and he stared at Tommy, his body trembling.

"You can do this. If you don't, you'll regret it. This is your chance for justice."

"J-Justice? No disrespect, Mr. Tittoti, but I've been down that road. Got a year and a half in juvie."

Tommy leaned forward, resting his forearms on his thighs. "I promise you, Ollie, you'll have your justice. If not by MASC, then by my hand." Claws shot from his fingertips to emphasize his point. "Do you believe me?"

"I . . . I want to." Ollie swallowed.

"If he says he'll give you justice, he will," I added. Tommy had never lied.

Ollie slowly uncurled his fingers from my jacket. "Okay. I know you won't steer me wrong, Alpha."

A kick in the chest couldn't have been more powerful. Leadership. That's what he needed from me.

"You have my word, too, Ollie. We're gonna settle up." And I meant it. When Tommy had told me we'd be coming, I'd been so angry I hadn't considered the larger picture.

Tommy chuckled. "Don't think about it too much, sugar. Trust me."

While part of me wanted to scoff, I didn't actually do it. I mean, what idiot trusted a demon?

Me. I was that idiot. I trusted him.

He wouldn't hurt me. He'd also shown he wouldn't let anyone else hurt me. I swallowed. Could I offer the same? Fuck yeah, or I'd die trying. I drew on my new alpha strength, sent calming energy Ollie's way. His shoulders unhunched from up near his ears, and he exhaled. Wow, I'd never tried that trick before. Cool.

Michael pulled up in front of the visitor center. I didn't wait for him to come around to the door. I threw it open and climbed out, pulling Ollie after me. Tommy stepped from the limo like a diva from some fucking fashion mag—one I'd probably beat off to as a teen—and brushed at nonexistent lint. He straightened his shoulders and nodded to me. I strode to his side with Ollie only a step behind.

We crossed into a visitor center that had a curved zinc façade that meshed into brick. I think it was supposed to be like a flag waving in the wind, or some such symbolism shit, but couldn't be sure. A bored-looking girl dressed in red-and white-striped leggings, a blue blouse, and a vest that looked like the flag, sighed upon seeing us.

"Sorry, the fort's closed." She picked at her cuticles. "It's not all that impressive, anyway."

"Kira!" A middle-aged woman wearing the same getup as the girl approached, her smile *waaay* too big to be genuine. Her name badge said "Jeannie."

"Don't mind her. Teens mean well, but they don't understand the national pride we have in our illustrious history. Come to see the fort, didja?" She continued smiling.

Ollie inched behind me. What was up with her? She didn't sound like a Baltimorean. And her smile told me there was no way in hell she was local.

"We've an appointment with Garrett Raggnarsson," Tommy said, completely unfazed. He handed her a card.

"Oh! Lucky you. Mr. Raggnarsson is such a gentleman. I can walk you that way if you'd like." Her smile never faltered, even after she glanced at the card.

"That won't be necessary. Thank you." Tommy moved past her. I shrugged and followed. Ollie accidentally bumped her as he stayed on my heels.

"Ope, sorry!" the woman called. "Have a good meeting!"

"What's wrong with her?" Ollie whispered.

Tommy sniggered. "She's from the Midwest. They're polite there."

"Weird." Ollie glanced back over his shoulder. "She's still smiling. And she just waved." He half-heartedly waved back.

I knew from past experience the fort lay at the end of a well-tended path, with the occasional bench and cherry tree growing alongside. We followed it along until we'd reached the fort, then walked through to the center courtyard.

"I've never been here," Ollie kept his voice quiet, like we were in church or something.

Maybe we were. Francis Scott Key had penned "The Star Spangled Banner" while watching the fort successfully defend Baltimore from British warships.

Our legacy.

I pointed to the two-story rectangular brick buildings. "Those were barracks." The posts, railings, and doors had a fresh coat of white paint, and the green shutters also had recently received some TLC. "I don't know if you can see it, but if we were on top of one of the buildings, you'd see the brick berms surrounding us are in the shape of a five-pointed star."

"Very good, sugar. That's the shape of the room we'll be entering for the commission, too. Five Rogers. Coincidence?" Tommy slid his hands in his pockets and seemed content to let Ollie look around.

"I thought maybe we were meeting right here in the open space." I looked around. No tables or anything that we could use for a meeting.

Tommy nodded toward the red brick vaulted structure between two barracks. The powder magazine. A structure that had held the powder and ammunition.

"We're meeting in there?" Too tight a space for too big egos.

"Sure are, shug." Tommy wandered in that direction, so Ollie and I followed. He stepped through an open white door and into an archway. A four-paneled red door with black bars in each of the panels was shut and locked. Tommy placed his hand against the door. It glowed, then swung open.

We stepped inside. Unlike the outside, wood planking covered the floor and walls, and a large display of wooden powder kegs and ammo boxes—I think for cannons—sat behind a rope barrier.

Tommy walked to the rope barrier, stepped over, and tapped on one of the powder kegs.

The ground shook. Ollie and I stumbled and reached for the wall to steady ourselves. What the hell?

24

The next thing I knew, we stood in a vaulted hallway with a door at the end. I blinked. How had that happened? Magic, obviously. But one second we were in one place and now here. Wherever the hell here actually was.

"You coming?" Tommy strode down the hall, command in every step.

We followed.

Tommy knocked on a heavy metal door with intricate runes carved along the edges.

"What do the runes do?" I ran a finger lightly over one. Since nothing exploded, I could assume they were safe to touch.

Tommy shook his head in despair, like he knew what I was thinking.

Bird of action, not so much brains.

"Well, shug, they disappear silver. Rings, bracelets, bullets. Too many creatures affected by the metal to allow it in our meeting space."

"What about magic?"

Tommy gave me a lopsided grin. "No Roger would show if they couldn't use their magic."

That seemed . . . stupid. But what did I know?

After I finished feeling up the runes, he opened the

door, and we entered. Just like he'd said, the room really was arranged in a five-pointed star. Like Fort McHenry. Someone had placed five separate tables, with three chairs each, near the points. The center of the star held a large round table with a map of Baltimore engraved into its top. Glowing purple lines marked the Neighborhoods—including Tommy's. A metal disk surrounded the bottom of the table like a spool. It anchored the legs of the chairs to it. Took me a minute to realize it wasn't my imagination—the center table rotated like a merry-go-round, only at a snail's pace. Talk about vomit-inducing.

"Ah, Tommy! Thanks for coming early," a deep bass rumbled from one corner of the room. "You can leave the door open."

Garrett Raggnarsson stepped into the light. Whoa. A griffin shifter. I'd never seen one before. His face was arresting, with a strong nose, a stronger jaw, and eyes that resembled those of an eagle, his gaze intense. Garret's hair hung to his shoulders and unlike Tommy's golden blond, it glowed almost white. Even had a single braid on one side that he'd woven through with a leather thong. At six feet, I still had to crane my neck to meet his gaze. Instead of a suit, he wore a tunic and leggings with two large metal bracers on his wrists, like he was straight out of a Tolkien movie. This guy would rock cosplay.

"How are you, Garrett? Long time no see, hon." Tommy walked up to the huge shifter, held out his hand, which Garrett immediately engulfed in his much larger one.

"I was hoping to keep it that way."

"Aww, now, you're going to hurt my feelings." Tommy chuckled.

Garrett snorted. "So, you think it's time?"

"I do."

"How many?" Garrett let go of Tommy's hand.

"Two, possibly three. You read my report."

"I did. . . . Who's that gorgeous creature?" Garrett said, nodding in Ollie's and my direction.

"Watch it, Garrett." Tommy's magic crackled. "Friend or not, Poe's off limits to your appetites."

But Garrett stepped around me and stood before Ollie, who gazed at the floor. Poor kid was probably scared senseless.

Garrett placed a finger under Ollie's chin and tipped it up. "Hey, sweetheart," he said in a gentle lilt. "What's your name?"

Ollie shuddered.

"You're scaring the kid. Leave him alone," I snapped. Ollie didn't need any more assholes making him feel small.

"I'm not scaring you, am I, pretty bird?" He crouched down to Ollie's height.

"N-No." Ollie's cheeks pinked.

"Hey, did you hear me? Back off Ollie. He's had a rough time." I didn't care if he was with MASC, the guy didn't need to be a slimy asshole. Tommy gripped my wrist.

"Shug, leave them. Trust me, he won't hurt Ollie." His eyes glinted, calculating.

What did he know that I didn't? I returned my attention to Ollie and Garrett. They remained in some weird stare off.

Footsteps sounded in the hallway. We all turned to look. I grabbed Ollie's elbow and pulled him to my side as a guy who looked like he belonged in a Matrix movie strode down the hall. Two sleek, female panther shifters followed him. All of them in leather with swords strapped to their backs. Kennedy would approve. The guy wore a large gold hoop in his nose with a chain that ran from the ring to his ear. A red Indian-silk scarf provided the only pop of color in his dark ensemble. His heavy brows, black eyes, and sharply trimmed beard gave him a sensual vibe he obviously played up.

Bengal Damon-Cowles. He wasn't a shifter exactly. Didn't quite smell like one, either, though I could swear I detected the faint whiff of catnip. I'd heard of Rakshasa, but he didn't look like a half-tiger half-man creature.

He stepped into the room. His features morphed until he resembled a tiger shifter stuck in a partial transformation. A tiger's head, but a black beard instead of white fur on his chin. He kept his humanoid form, though his hands had sprouted claws and fur. Stripes disappeared under his clothing.

"Garrett, this is truly out of line. We already had our annual meeting. Dragging us here again is unconscionable. And boring." He inspected his claws.

"Is it me, or does he sound like Shere Khan from *The Jungle Book*?" Ollie whispered.

Bengal snorted, his ears twitching. "I have been a muse for many, bird." His eyes fastened on Tommy. "I wondered if you would show. How . . . delightful."

"You know me, Ben. I'm here when needed." Tommy laced his words with meaning.

"Indeed." Bengal introduced his companions. Tommy introduced me and Ollie. Ben placed his hands together in front of his chest to greet Garrett, then moved to one of the five tables.

"Where are we gonna sit?" I asked. There were five tables and five Rogers. Tommy might have a Neighborhood, but he wasn't a Roger. Or at least that seemed to be the consensus.

"We'll be at the center table with Garrett, birdie. All eyes on us." He didn't seem intimidated by it. Or the spinning. I grimaced.

Next came Josephine Jones and two vampires who looked like androgynous bookends. They dressed in black with large sunhats and prominent netting. Soon, we'd have enough for a rave. The vampires moved with inhuman grace, blending into the shadows, appearing and disappearing too quickly for the eye to track. Josephine greeted Tommy, Bengal, and Garrett while ignoring the rest of us. She chose the point with the dimmest lighting and the vampires blended into the corner's shadow.

The Hons soon followed, Angel Pingelton and her two enforcers all wearing towering beehive hairdos, matching unzipped Pink Ladies jackets, and sparkly cat-eye glasses. Her fairy enforcers wore housedresses under their jackets, while Angel wore a poodle skirt and a tight white sweater. Looked like they stepped off the set of *Hairspray*. How did they get their sparkly wings through the fabric of the jackets? Their wings fluttered as they moved, their feet just brushing the floor.

The Coven came next. Susannah Moore had long, plaited brown hair and plain features. She and the other two mages wore earth-toned clothing with runes stitched into the fabric. Honestly, they looked like they should sell candles at a Ren Fest or some such shit. But since she was almost as powerful a mage as her husband had been, looks were deceiving.

Susannah gasped when she saw Tommy, and the hair on my arms rose when she pulled magic around her.

Tommy grinned, his posture straightening. If he'd been a cat, his tail would have been twitching.

"Stand down, Susannah," Garrett said, the griffin's voice deepening to a threatening growl. "Not the time."

After a tense second, she released her magic. She glared daggers at Tommy. He grinned, letting his eyes shift for a moment. A warning. Her mage enforcers hustled her toward their table.

Minutes passed before Briggs, Andre, and . . . Ethan entered. Briggs wore a snakeskin-patterned purple suit with a white pocket square and white wingtips. He looked relaxed. Too relaxed. Andre wore his usual ill-fitting suit and smug grin, but his firepower was noticeably missing, replaced by a dagger at his hip. And Ethan . . . no snakehead badge on his suit. His eyes could have bored holes through me.

I waved and would have taunted him further, but Ollie paled, his breath coming in sudden wheezes. I pulled him closer and sent out alpha calm. Surprisingly, Garrett stepped to his other side and placed a hand on Ollie's shoulder. Ollie instantly stopped shaking, and his breathing evened out.

I could swear I heard a low growl rumble from Garrett's chest. What the hell? I'd be asking Tommy just exactly what he saw when he looked at Garrett—later.

Briggs greeted the room, his voice jovial, then he and his crew took their seats.

Garrett nodded and indicated that we should sit. I grimaced but didn't complain about the spinning table. He waited until Tommy, Ollie, and I sat, then perched on the edge of the table.

"As you know, I've called a special commission today to address some grievances between the Rogers—"

"I thought perhaps we could handle our business privately?" Bengal broke in. "Surely, we do not need to waste a day on this and MASC's valuable time."

Garrett groaned. "Yes, Ben, my time *is* valuable, so please don't waste it with pointless interruptions. If I may continue?"

"Certainly." Bengal settled back into his seat, folding his hands across his belly.

Asshole. But I hid a smirk because I'd do the same thing in his position.

"Josephine Jones has pressed a case against Briggs Bickley. I understand that Tommy Tittoti would also like to introduce a complaint against Briggs."

"He's *not* a Roger. Why are you entertaining his complaint?" Susannah snarled.

"Tommy, you said your complaint relates to Josephine's, correct?" Garrett asked.

"Yes."

"Then I'll allow it." Garrett held up a hand to keep the Coven from protesting. Still, muttering broke out among the Rogers. The Hons sat forward in their chairs, while Bengal's crew looked bored. Briggs still seemed too confident for his position, Andre looked like he wanted to fight everyone, and my stepdad looked like he'd be ill at any moment. Fucking coward.

"Any other cases to consider?" Garrett scanned the assembly as we continued to rotate. I didn't trust having my back to Briggs. Would have felt much more comfortable in my raven form taking up a perch in the rafters.

I could feel the hatred coming our way from the Coven. I'm sure they wanted to address Tommy killing Obrum Drach, but since it had happened in Josephine's territory, Susannah couldn't do so without explaining what he was doing illegally in another Roger's Neighborhood.

"Then I turn the floor over to Josephine." Garrett waved in her direction.

Josephine detached herself from the shadows, her gaze

taking in all the Rogers before settling on Briggs' table. "Briggs Bickley trespassed in my Neighborhood and claimed three blocks as his own. He sent machinery to demolish the buildings there. He allowed his people into my Neighborhood without consequence. I demand redress." She flashed her fangs at Briggs.

"Now, now, darling, I have a contract." Briggs snapped his fingers, and Andre pulled a rolled-up paper from his suit. Andre approached our table, and Ollie clamped onto my knee in a bruising grip. Garrett didn't miss the gesture if his narrowing eyes were any sign. But Andre simply handed the contract to Garrett and retreated without a single glance Ollie's way.

Garrett scanned the document, nodded. "You claim Ethan Short sold you the properties, Briggs. This is highly unusual. If we allow anyone to sell off their properties in someone else's Neighborhood, we'd soon find pieces carved out of everyone's territories."

"It abuts my Neighborhood, anyway. Plus, I have a signed affidavit from Mr. Short claiming neglect. Seems Josephine hadn't bothered to keep the lights on in this part of town. No working street lamps, no power after dark, sporadic power otherwise."

"Lies—" Josephine bared her fangs again, leaned over the table. Ethan stepped behind Andre.

Not so bold now that I had all his alpha power.

"Is it any wonder Mr. Short would want to sell to me?" Briggs held his hands up in a "what can you do" gesture.

"Except that he's lying." I'd kept quiet until now, but I wasn't gonna let Ethan lie without consequence. "I lived in those blocks and so did Ollie, and we'll both testify we had no issues with power."

"Out of order," Bengal called. "Non-Rogers shouldn't speak unless asked a direct question."

Dick.

"Granted." Garrett turned to me. "Poe, did you live in the three blocks that Briggs' purchased?"

"Yes." See, I could stick with the program.

"And did you have the issues Mr. Short is claiming?"

"Nope." I added a little extra pop to the 'p' just to be an asshole.

"What say you, Mr. Short? Explain yourself."

I could hear Ethan's painful swallow from here. He inched out from behind Andre. "Poe Dupin is my stepson, Your, uh, Honor. I took care of him even after his mama died. He's a troubled man and has issues with me. He recently stole my roost away. I wouldn't take anything he says as true."

"Fuck. You." I even flipped him the bird.

Garrett shushed me, while Tommy coughed into his hand.

"Charming," Bengal added.

"Would you be okay with some asshole lying about you?" I asked. "Ethan lost his roost because he was a piss-poor alpha, a drunkard, a gambler, and a fucking loser. And now a liar. I didn't steal them, they came to me."

"Immaterial," Susannah snapped. "Why are we listening to nobodies? Briggs purchased the land from that raven fair and square. If Josephine doesn't take care of her areas, then why shouldn't he take the area to develop?"

"It's mine—" Josephine began.

"I agree." Tommy sat back in his chair, crossed his arms. "Briggs has a legitimate contract."

"What?" Josephine screeched. "You can't mean that!"

"A contract's a contract. A demon respects a deal. Even a poor one." He shrugged.

What the hell was he up to? No way he'd turn on Josephine. Would he?

The Hons muttered among themselves, and Josephine looked like she'd rip Tommy to shreds if she were daring enough to try.

Bengal laughed. "Ooh, this is becoming entertaining after all." He leaned back in his chair and put his boots up on the table, settling in.

"Not helping," Angel Pingelton snapped, her cat-eye glasses sliding down her nose.

"Whoever said I needed to be helpful?" Bengal scoffed.

"Order!" Garrett slammed his fist on the table. The purple lines shifted, and Briggs' territory seemed to merge into the ravens' blocks.

"I call a vote," Angel pursed her lips, her beehive wobbling. "I vote the land is Josephine's."

"Yes, I vote for myself, too," Josephine nodded.

Briggs sighed. "I vote for myself. I have a contract. Even the demon admits it."

"Agreed," Susannah nodded. "I vote Briggs."

All heads turned Bengal's way. He focused on his claws, not saying a word. When he glanced up, he smirked. "Abstain."

Most everyone groaned. Tommy chuckled, and Garrett pinched the bridge of his nose.

"I'm so glad Briggs is all about the contract," Tommy pretended to search his pockets, "Because then he'll understand why burning down other people's property is wrong. I believe there's an ownership contract—" he kept patting until he finally pulled out a deed and placed it on the table

—"in place. Correct me if I'm wrong, but that means the owner has a right to challenge."

Garrett frowned at Tommy. "No citizen has a right to challenge a Roger over property in their Neighborhood. And you acknowledge it's his."

"Citizen? Ha, no, you misunderstand me. If you'll look at the contract, you'll notice I own 51 percent of Spun Gold. So, the way I see it, Briggs attacked *my* territory and *my* worker. Do I need to remind you, Garrett, that I have an agreement with MASC that I can vigorously defend my territory?" He grinned, all fang.

The room fell silent.

Oh, shit, here we go!

25

"But you're not able to expand your territory," Garrett sputtered. "So even if you own the building, you can't count it as part of your Neighborhood."

"Agreed." Briggs slammed his hand on the table as if putting the final nail in Tommy's claim.

My anger boiled, but I reined it in when Tommy grinned. "Ah, no, Garrett, you've got it wrong. I can't *seek* to expand my territory. Poe came to me to bargain. He'll confirm."

I nodded.

"You should read our contract, hon. The devil—or in this case, demon—is in the details." He patted his pockets again and pulled out another document. "Ah, I happen to have it with me."

He handed it to Garrett.

"Of course you do." Garrett looked like he'd swallowed a lemon as he scanned the document. "Son of a bitch."

"Probably. I never knew my mother, but you know how we demons roll." Tommy stood. "The way I see it, Briggs has two options. He can either acknowledge the territory as his, which in turn makes Spun Gold my territory. If so, I demand my right to collect his soul. And the pig's, too. He's the one who attacked my employee and left him for dead. Ollie can confirm this." Tommy ran his tongue along his bottom lip.

I'm almost embarrassed to say it gave me a hard on. Fuck, he was hot when he was about to kill someone.

"Alternatively," Tommy offered, "Briggs can agree that he trespassed on Josephine's territory and did damage to her Neighborhood. He'll have to reimburse her for the costs, and MASC will need to fine him as well for his blatant attempt to unfairly liberate another Roger's territory. I believe the price of incursion is offering a piece of his territory of equal size to Josephine. Briggs, I'm good either way, just let me know which one you choose." His smile became sharp.

Briggs gaped.

Fuck, that was pure brilliance. I could have kissed him.

Bengal belly laughed. "Excellent play, Tommy. You always manage to surprise me."

"That's not fair." Susannah pointed to Briggs. "We have a contract. We're going to open a casino on that land in a joint venture."

"Ah, you can't do that unless Briggs' claims ownership. Otherwise, it's not his to contract. You can lodge a complaint, but since he'll be dead . . ." Tommy shrugged.

Garrett stood to his full height. "Tommy has a point. So, which is it Briggs? Let's finish this."

Trapped like a fucking rat on a sinking ship. I swear I smelled the bitter stank of his fear.

Briggs stared at the table, his expression blank. Everyone waited for his decision, breath held. When he whipped his head upward, his eyes shot their lasers right at Tommy. Both beams struck him in the face, and Tommy turned to stone.

Damn. No matter that Tommy had the necklace, it still

stopped my heart to see him become stone. I hoped he fucking knew what he was doing.

I grabbed Ollie and shoved him under the table. Briggs turned his gaze on Garrett, but his beam ricocheted off one of Garrett's bracers like some Wonder Woman shit and struck one of the Hons. The fairy turned to stone.

"Kill Garrett!" Briggs ordered Ethan and Andre. "Without the demon doing their dirty work, MASC won't have any power here."

The Hons had thrown some fairy magic at Briggs, but it didn't strike. The Coven launched a mini-sun at the vampires, who fell back as far as they could into their corner. Then the Hons attacked the Coven. Briggs strode toward us.

It was on.

I ducked under the table so Briggs' gaze wouldn't fall on me. I could see Tommy's legs. Still stone. But his shadow became a thing of nightmares. Cloven hooves, a long, barbed tail, horns, and wings that reminded me of a bat's. The shadow thrashed, even as Tommy remained frozen.

"Stay here, Ollie." I transformed into my raven form and launched myself from under the table. Ethan, in raven form as well, dove at Garrett's head, trying to distract him, as Garrett defended himself from Andre's blade and Briggs' laser vision.

When my good-for-nothing stepdad swooped once again, I intercepted, banging into him and sending him spinning out of control. He crashed onto the floor at the foot of Bengal's table. The Rakshasa remained seated, feet still propped, watching the action. It wouldn't have surprised me if he'd brought popcorn. His panther guards took up on either side of his table, their swords drawn. I circled back around.

The Demon's in the Details | 199

The Hons and Coven traded magical blows, neither gaining much on the other. One vampire had already turned to ash under the mini-sun, while Josephine and another curled into tight balls, writhing. The smell of burning flesh reminded me of Ollie. I squawked. Not on my watch.

I raced toward the mini-sun, hoping it wasn't actually hot. I raked my claws through it as I passed. The spell dissolved. The vampires instantly sprang up and raced toward the Coven, who now had to defend themselves from both fairies and enraged vampires. Not my problem.

Garrett was still holding his own, but defending against Briggs' attacks meant he left himself open to Andre's blade. Before I could join the fray, a loud *crack* sounded. I squawked, familiar with the sound of Briggs' spell breaking.

Tommy threw off the stone and stepped from the rubble, his sights set on Briggs. He roared. Bloodcurdling. Inhuman. Apex Predator among prey.

Everyone froze.

Tommy's shadow thrashed. His magic surrounded him in a swirling mass, his eyes fiery red.

Oh, Briggs had really pissed off Tommy.

Andre lunged for Garrett, who was as enraptured as everyone else by Tommy's display of sheer power. I screeched in warning, too late! But Andre tripped . . . no, Ollie had tackled his legs. Garrett spun and thrust his eagle talons through Andre's chest as the boar shifter fell into him. The talons protruded through Andre's back. That had to hurt. Couldn't happen to a nicer pig.

As much as I wanted to enjoy Andre's death throes, I had bigger fish—er, snakes—to fry.

Tommy stalked Briggs as everyone watched. Briggs backed up, but he'd never escape. He fumbled in his pocket and pulled out . . . my crystal cube.

A collective gasp rose from the group. Everyone but me seemed to know what it was.

"Found this in your boyfriend's safe, demon." Briggs held it aloft. It pulsed as an inky smoke swirled from it.

What the hell was it?

Tommy took a step back, his face draining of color. I'd never seen him afraid before.

"Say hello to hell for me." Briggs laughed.

I dove. Snatched the cube from his hand and shot for the rafters.

I couldn't see Briggs' expression, but when I circled back, I saw Tommy's. Gleeful. He strode toward Briggs. Briggs kept shooting his lasers at Tommy, but this time Tommy absorbed it, his magic swelling with each strike. Briggs turned and tried to run, but Tommy sprung, landing on Briggs' back. He reached around and placed his hand on Briggs' chest.

Briggs' screamed. Pure agony. He shook, and froth spilled from his mouth as Tommy yanked his soul from him, like peeling the skeleton out in one go. Briggs continued to scream as Tommy forcefully pulled his magic from him. He fell, and Tommy came down on top. Tommy's shadow mimicked devouring the Briggs-shaped magic. As it disappeared into the shadow's huge maw, Briggs' body shimmered and turned to salt.

The cube no longer pulsed in my talons. I wasn't sure what to do with it, so I stayed aloft, watching from above. Tommy rose as a commotion by the door caught my attention. Bengal had Susannah by the throat, his fangs buried in her shoulder. She struggled, but he held tight.

Tommy approached. She threw a blast of magic his way. He swallowed it and kept coming. "Thanks, Susannah. I would have been required to let you live. Not now."

Before she could react, his magic zinged, and she turned into salt, her magic shooting into him.

Bengal brushed at his clothing. "Expect the bill for the cleaning, demon. At least, I believe my debt is paid."

"It is indeed."

Bengal nodded. "Freedom is a beautiful thing."

"Nice doing business with you, Ben. Remember, if you ever need anything..."

He held up his hands. "Not unless I must."

"You never know."

Bengal snorted. "Garrett, can I conclude that we're done here? Unless you plan to divide Coven and Briggs' territory, of course. Then I will willingly stay."

"Nice try, Ben." Garrett stood with Ollie at his side, his large arm draped over Ollie's shoulders. "I'll let the rest of you know MASC's decisions in the coming days. We've had enough for today."

Bengal didn't ask questions. He and his panthers exited.

The Hons and vampires were worse for the wear. Angel's beehive listed to one side, and she'd lost her glasses along the way. Her jacket was singed in several places. The other fairies had lost their lives defending her, but they'd wiped out all the mages. Josephine and another vampire remained standing with blood around their mouths.

Tommy walked among the dead, his magic settling around him and retreating inside. Josephine and Angel clasped forearms before turning to nod to Tommy, then Garrett. They exited the room together. Ethan had disappeared. Had he seen what happened to Briggs or had he fled before that?

"You can come down now, shug," Tommy called. His expression looked...troubled, his face pinched.

Had he somehow been hurt?

26

I swooped down and transformed as soon as I landed, the cube clutched in my fist.

"You want to be real careful with that, Poe." Garrett grinned and inched my way. "In fact, you might want to hand it over. I'll take care of it for you."

"Nice try. Think I'll hold on to it."

Garrett sighed. "Can't blame a griffin for trying. You have no idea what it is, do you?"

"Garrett." Tommy gave him a pointed look.

"What? The guy's got a right to know he's got you by the short and curlies. It's not everyday someone gets the jump on you."

Tommy's jaw clenched.

"Is it dangerous?" Ollie asked.

"In a manner of speaking, pretty bird. Why don't we give these two some time alone to sort this out?" Garrett held out his elbow to Ollie.

"Alpha?" Ollie looked between me and Tommy, his bottom lip caught between his teeth. He didn't look all that shook up that he'd watched Andre die. Then again, if someone set me on fire, I probably wouldn't be overly upset at their demise either.

"You okay, Ollie?" I couldn't let him go if he needed me. "You don't have to go."

Garrett raised a brow but wisely kept his mouth shut.

"Oh, no, it's okay. I'd like to get out of this room. It smells." He wrinkled his nose.

Huh. I really thought he'd be a mess. But his face looked as relaxed as I'd seen it since . . . well, since I'd met him. Maybe it was a griffin thing. Like how rakshasas were irresistible to cat shifters. Maybe griffins were the same for birds. Though I certainly didn't feel the pull.

"We'll be out soon," I said.

Ollie nodded and placed his arm through Garrett's and tentatively smiled up at him. They left, Ollie leaning into Garrett.

"Should I worry about that?" I asked.

"Garrett's intentions aren't nefarious, if that's what you're asking."

"Hmmm." I side-eyed Tommy. He stared at the floor, a line forming between his eyebrows. I faced him. "What gives? What is this thing?"

He grimaced but met my gaze. "It's a . . . banishment cube. I'd thought I'd destroyed them all, but every so often, one pops up."

"Will it hurt you?"

"It can send me back through the rift." A muscle in his jaw ticked. "You should use it to bargain for your freedom. I'll give you anything for it."

"Why are you telling me this?" That alone made me suspicious.

"I'm trying to give you a way out, shug. You don't want to be trapped. That holds your freedom."

"And if I keep it?"

Pain flashed across Tommy's face before his expression went blank. "Then you'd have the upper hand. Eventually,

MASC would try to take it. It's too valuable to leave with you. But for a while, you'd be in control."

"And that worries you?"

"That MASC would hurt you in the process? Yes."

Really? "You know what I'm asking. Would you be upset if I kept it?"

"Yes." His voice came out tiny. "I'll never be safe with it in existence."

Such a small crystal cube. I carefully turned it over in my palm, the lettering familiar but still not spelling any word I knew.

"So, if I use it to bargain, I can ask for my freedom, and you'd grant it?"

"It would be more than a generous trade in my favor. It would delight my nature." He swallowed. "You could, of course, ask for more."

I blinked. He kept telling me to ask for more. Why? That went against everything in his nature.

Holy shit! Lightning couldn't strike this hard. Kennedy was right. *He fucking loved me.* Me, a scruffy bird from the wrong side of Baltimore. A lump rose in my throat.

"Shug?"

"There's only one problem with your plan."

"What's that?"

"I don't want you to let me go."

"What? You—"

I placed the cube on the floor, raised my boot, and stomped. The cube shattered underneath my heel.

Tommy's mouth fell open, and his eyes widened comically. He pointed at my boot. "You . . . you just . . ."

"Took care of a threat to you. Yeah, guess I did."

"Poe—"

"I'm yours. Probably was from the first time I saw you. Just took me a while to figure it out. Or that you'd want me."

"Oh, shug, that's *never* been in question."

"Well, I'm a little slow. I only now figured it out."

Tommy raked a hand through his hair. "It's not that I don't want you. It's that I *do*. Poe, my nature is *greedy*. I want you in my bed every night. I want to pamper you, and wreck you, and . . . there's not quite a word for it in this world, but 'mate' comes closest."

"Like wolf shifters do?" Ravens didn't have the same concept. We married but didn't have the mating instinct like some shifters. Though come to think on it, I didn't know of a single divorced raven couple. Huh.

"Oh, no, sugar. That bond can be broken. If one partner dies, the other sometime survives. That wouldn't be the case with us."

"But I'll only live 200 years or so." Why would he give up his life for such a short time with me?

Tommy shook his head. "No. Your life span would match mine. You'd watch your roost grow old, and you'd know their grandchildren's grandchildren. Indefinitely. You'd suffer loss. It's not easy."

Fuck. "But we'd be together?"

"Yes. There'd be no separating us. Not that we'd want to be. That's a side effect of the bond. Our feelings would only deepen."

"Huh."

"You need time to think about it, and I'll understand if it's too much—"

"How do we do it?"

"It's a ritual."

"Like a sex ritual?" I waggled my eyebrows.

Tommy rolled his eyes. "Preferably. But it's not something to joke about. You'd be mine forever in a way you aren't now."

"But you'd be mine, too, right? It wouldn't only be me in this?"

"No, sugar, we'd both be in it together."

I drew in a sudden breath. "Let's do it."

∽

Tommy clasped my elbow in a steely grip and dragged me back to the car, with Ollie jogging to keep up. We'd barely said goodbye to Garrett, who seemed pretty amused by it all. Like he knew something I didn't.

Michael pulled up to the curb. By the time we reached it, he had opened the door. First, Tommy waved Ollie inside. Then he didn't quite shove me inside . . . but he shoved me inside . . . before climbing in behind and sitting across from me. His eyes kept switching from violet to red, and he'd clenched his fists. Must be something I said.

And because I couldn't help myself, I licked my bottom lip. Tommy's eyes turned blistering, and he glared at me. I grinned. Then pressed my ankle against his.

He jerked away like I'd electrocuted him. Shook his head in warning. Ooh, what fun. I slouched in my seat, made sure to manspread. I mean, a guy needed some room, right? The look he gave could have burned me to ash.

Ollie cleared his throat. We both startled. Oh, yeah, Ollie.

"What's up, kid?" I asked.

He held up his phone. "Mom and Dad want to know if we can keep the twins tonight? They've been making some sort of cake and watching movies."

I'd given the Clemms an overnight bag for the kids in

case Ollie and I returned late. Since it was only dinnertime, I assumed he suggested they have the kids sleep over. Ollie was good people.

"Yeah, sure. Sounds good. But what, oh, what will I do with all those lonely hours?"

Tommy huffed and turned to look out the window, his jaw clenched.

I decided not to taunt him further and chatted with Ollie until we pulled up to our apartment building. Ollie climbed out, then waved. He truly seemed unbothered by all the carnage today. I'd have to check in with him... tomorrow.

As I went to pull the door closed, Tommy stopped me. "Shug, you should go. Take some time to think. This is a big thing, and I—"

I narrowed my eyes. Huh. A demon with cold feet. "You can read my desires, right? So, you tell me, do I look unsure?"

"You're impulsive—"

"Decisive."

"I'll wreck you."

"Hell yeah! And you think that's gonna discourage me?" I pulled the door closed. "Hey, Michael, put up the divider, would ya?"

I waited for him to do so. Then we set off toward Tommy's place.

"We're not having sex in the limo." Tommy crossed his arms.

A demon pouting. Who woulda thunk it? "Agreed. I want a bed."

Tommy huffed.

"Don't worry, we might not even have sex tonight. I mean, I don't just give this ass away." Okay, I had in the past, but we were talking the here and now. "And you know, if we mate, or whatever, you're gonna be a step-parent. I'm not willing to be with a guy who won't take care of my kids."

Tommy's jaw popped open. "What?"

"You heard me. You want my ass for all eternity, I've got conditions you'll need to meet."

"Are you . . . bargaining with me?" Tommy's eyes went wide.

I smirked. "Maybe."

Come on, come on . . .

He leaned forward, placed his elbows on his knees. "It's not smart to deal with a demon, shug. You should know that by now."

"I'm a slow learner. So, as I was saying, you'd have to be a good stepparent. I'd expect you to be involved. And they need to go to college. If they want, I mean. I wouldn't force them."

"And that's all?" Tommy pursed his lips. Disappointment?

"You mentioned pampering me, right?"

His eyes flashed red again. "I did."

"Yeah, I'd want a lot of that. And not just on my birthday, either. I don't want to be taken for granted. And I don't mean the material things. Quality time, date nights, all that shit. Family time."

Oh, this was fun.

"Uh-huh." Tommy's lips turned up in the hint of a smile. "What else?"

"Um, I'm a simple bird. I want my roost looked after properly. Most of that I can do myself, but I'd like your support when necessary."

"My, aren't you a romantic, birdie? Family, friends, and nice dinners. A white picket fence perhaps?"

"Nah, I like your penthouse just fine."

"Well, shug, since you're in the mood to bargain," he flashed a hint of fang at me, "I have a few conditions of my own."

"Oh, yeah? More than my ass for eternity? Hmmm, I'm not so sure. I'm offering you an awful lot."

"More than you know. But I'm possessive by nature. Once . . . mated, I'd want a sign that you belong to me."

"Like what? A collar? Kinky, but I'm not down with it. That's a dog thing."

Tommy leaned back in his seat. "Definitely not a collar. It would be something that only you and I would see."

"Like a tattoo? Or piercing? Ooh, a tramp stamp. Only I'd get to veto the wording. No 'Tommy's Slut' or anything trashy."

Tommy snorted. "No, I promise you, nothing trashy."

"What if I say no?"

"Then I wouldn't make you."

"I might not like the symbolism of being owned. Free bird, remember? It's kinda my thing." I hummed a few bars of Lynyrd Skynyrd.

"You do. And it's really not." Tommy looked me up and down like he was confirming his statements. Damn, having a guy who could read my desires was hot but kind of annoying, too. And he wasn't wrong. Just talking about keeping something between the two of us appealed to my nature. And my dick.

"As long as I have veto power if I don't like it, I'd be okay with that."

"I'd never make you do something you hated, sugar. I want to make you so happy that you'll never regret being with me."

I liked the sound of that. By his grin, he knew exactly how his words affected me.

When Michael pulled into the private parking lot, he'd barely put the limo in park before Tommy and I hopped out. Tommy waved me toward the elevator and stayed to talk to Michael. Within a minute, he joined me and placed his palm against the elevator plate. The moment the elevator doors opened, he grabbed my elbow and yanked me in after him. The doors slid closed, and I found myself pressed in a corner with Tommy's lips against mine.

"Mmph!" Not that I minded. Hell yeah, let's get the party started.

I didn't even notice when the doors opened, until Tommy tugged me out with him, keeping our lips connected. We broke apart, and he steered us toward his bedroom.

"Last chance, sugar. Once I get you in that room, I'm going to do nasty things to you until the early hours of the morning."

27

"Bring it." Tommy's dares only turned me on, anyway. And he knew it.

We stumbled into his room, and he shoved me down on the bed.

"Strip. Now." He dropped his suit jacket, then grabbed one of my boots and unlaced it.

Thunk! It hit the floor. Same with the next.

"Shug, I said to get naked. Do you want me to tear your clothes off?"

I swallowed. The imagery sent a jolt to my cock. But I loved my leather jacket and I didn't want to have to replace any more clothes. I tossed it onto the floor and started on my shirt.

He stood back and stripped off his tie, throwing it on a pillow. "We might need it later depending how you behave."

"How bad do I have to be to get you to use it?" I rolled away when he grabbed for my ankle. "Ah, ah, I'm not naked yet."

"Birdie, you don't want to tease me right now. I've been *very* patient."

"Maybe I don't want you to be patient." I shucked my jeans, underwear, and socks and rolled to my side, propping myself up on an elbow. "I'm waiting."

Tommy removed his shirt and pulled his belt off. He

added that to the pillow. Hot damn. He didn't rush to strip the rest off, taking his own sweet time. Tease. I loved it.

He wasn't wearing manties tonight, but his snug boxer briefs fit him like a glove. Once he removed them, he shut his eyes and took a deep breath. Shuddered.

"What's wrong?" I sat up.

"I don't want to push you too hard." He kept his eyes squeezed shut. "I'm a lot stronger than I look. I'm afraid I'll scare you."

"Demon, I've seen your shadow eat a Roger's soul. I know what you're capable of, and I know you won't hurt me. Bring it on. I want it. I want *you*."

When his eyes snapped open, they shone a scorching red, and his magic crackled around us. Yes, yes, hell to the yes.

He sank onto his knees on the bed and crawled to me. He ran a finger along the stubble on my jaw. "You're perfect for me, birdie. I knew it the first moment I saw you. You smelled of Kennedy's perfume, and I hated it. It's the reason I chose to shave you. I could cover you in one of my aftershaves."

"I thought you were an incubus because you made me so hard that I could barely think." I mean, as long as we were being honest.

Tommy chuckled, rich and dark.

I shivered.

"Hang on, sugar, I'm about to ruin you for all others." He leaned toward me, so slowly, his lips drawing close but pausing a hair's breadth from mine.

I leaned in and connected our mouths.

He kissed me softly, like I was precious. Just a brush of our lips before he pulled back.

"Wha—"

He slammed our lips back together, and his tongue swept into my mouth like a wave to the shore. Before I could even draw a breath, he stole it, pushed me back onto the pillows. His hand came to my throat, but he didn't squeeze, simply rested it there as he raided my mouth like it was some treasure trove. Fuck, he didn't give me time to think, his magic pouring into me, making me tingle. I wrapped my arms around his shoulders, holding on tight.

I'd wanted to know what he'd feel like inside me since we first met. When he broke our kiss, he tightened his hand on my throat slightly and lowered his mouth to my neck. He latched on and sucked up a mark. I tipped my chin back, giving him full access.

He growled and nipped my shoulder. I jerked, but damn, that was hot. I'd always liked a little pain with my pleasure.

Tommy ran his tongue down my collarbone and then, in one motion, slid down until he was between my legs. He nipped my thigh, then rested his forehead on it. Looked like he was in pain. I watched him struggle, his claws lengthening then retracting, a fine tremor to his body.

I didn't want him to be controlled. I liked his wild side. Wanted to experience it firsthand.

"Hey, demon boy. Get on with it. I'm about to fall asleep up here." That should do it.

His features morphed into something from a sci-fi horror movie: red mottled skin, elongated snout, thick, twisted horns, teeth-filled maw.

But only for a split second. If I had blinked, I'd have missed it. Maybe I should have been terrified. I wasn't. He belonged to me.

I'd never believed in all that fated mates crap. At least not for me. Always suspected it was bullshit other shifters made up to feel superior. But maybe, just maybe, there was something to it. Either way, I *chose* him, and that made him mine.

Before I could blab my feelings, I found myself flipped over with my ass in the air and my face smashed into a pillow.

Probably for the best.

Not sure where the lube came from, but when two slick fingers pushed inside me, I grunted, unprepared for it. The bite of pain quickly became pleasure as he rubbed me just right, his movements strong and sure. I spread my legs wider to give him more room to work and pushed my ass toward him. I didn't want a lot of prep. Wanted the first push into my body to be memorable.

A hand came down on my ass. Hard.

I yelped. I'd have a handprint-sized bruise later. Fuck, if he did that again, things would be over before they ever started. I concentrated on not blowing my load like a teenager on his first fuck.

Tommy soothed a hand over my ass, and I reached between my legs to pinch the tip of my cock. A little pain to take the edge off. He chuckled.

"So worked up, shug." He pressed his dick against my entrance and nudged, bounced off the rim. Tommy was trying to kill me. He did it again. I grumbled. He chuckled. Evil bastard. He applied a hint of pressure this time, slowly opening me up. Damn it. I wasn't a patient bird.

"I don't suppose demons knot like wolves?" I'd heard a knot could feel pretty amazing during sex, though the one time I'd gotten a guy to do it, I'd been rather meh about it.

He paused. "What?" His breath came out on a moan. He pushed a little harder.

"You know, a knot? On your dick."

"Sugar, you have the weirdest sex talk. No, no knotting."

"Oh, 'kay." I tried not to sound disappointed. I mean, a guy couldn't get everything, right?

Another hand came down on my ass. Other side this time.

I howled and tried to jerk away, but Tommy grabbed my hips and slammed into me. Oh, *fuuuck*. The burn. I cried out. Perfection. My body protested, clamping tight, even as I gloried in it.

"Shhh, birdie, you can take me." Tommy ran his hand over my back in a soothing motion.

"Move," I gritted out between clenched teeth. I didn't want sweet and nice. Wanted him to own my ass, make it his. I shoved back onto him, the bite of pain still there, but morphing into a pleasing fullness.

Tommy took the hint. He drew back, then pounded me into the mattress. He didn't show mercy, either.

Sounds I never thought I'd make spilled from my mouth, and I braced my hands against the headboard as he took everything my body gave and then some. He pegged my prostate repeatedly, each jab a mix of pleasure/pain. His grip on my hips kept me anchored even when I struggled.

When I bucked and almost threw him off, he growled low in his throat.

Oh shit, that was hot.

He gripped my wrist and pinned it behind my back. "Take it, sugar. You know you want to. You're opening up so nicely for me."

His voice had a rough edge that rubbed at all the raw places in my soul. I writhed under him, thrashed, unsure whether I wanted to get away or get closer. My knees scrabbled for purchase, but he widened his stance, and it removed whatever leverage I'd had. Curse words spilled from my mouth as his movements forced my back to bow.

And then I fucking mewled. Like a damn cat. Just yowled and couldn't seem to stop myself.

Shit, I seemed to learn something new about myself every time we were together. Later, I'd die of mortification, but for now, I let go, giving him my sounds and offering my body as tribute.

The smell of apples grew stronger, almost choking me. Yet, I couldn't get enough. I gasped, my chest expanding, apples and more apples making me lightheaded. Fuck, I wouldn't actually pass out, would I?

"More, more, more," I chanted. And he gave it.

"So, birdie." Tommy didn't even sound winded, while I felt like I'd run a marathon.

"Yeah?" I gasped out between thrusts, peeking over my shoulder at him.

He slammed his hips against me and stayed put. "I may not have a knot, but I do have barbs." He grinned, his fangs protruding.

Took my lust-drunk brain a moment to process. "Barbs?"

"Yeah, sugar. Holds you in place while I claim you and releases healing oils so we can go all night."

Sudden pain that felt like dozens of tiny needles simultaneously had me clamping down on him. Before I could do more than gasp, pleasure so strong I almost blacked out radiated from where we were connected. I burned. I ached. I writhed but couldn't get away from the swamping pleasure.

"That's right, sweetheart. Let me hear you." Tommy leaned forward and sank his fangs into my shoulder. I shouted. I could feel him pulsing inside me, his come scalding and yet so, so good. A tendril of his magic forced its way inside my mouth, down my throat, seemed to anchor itself in my chest.

I hope his room had soundproofing because I yelled

until I was hoarse. On the knife's edge of panic and desire, my back bowed and I turned my face into a pillow.

My vision went white, and everything drew tight before I shuddered and felt like my body was shaking apart. I came on the sheets, my ass clamped tight around Tommy's girth. His magic hummed, and I swear it felt . . . happy.

Tommy released my wrist but kept my hips anchored to his. I gulped in air, my hair matted from sweat. When I looked over my shoulder at him, his eyes remained a glowing red.

We stayed that way for a while, until I felt his body release mine. He pulled out slowly, and I slumped to the mattress. Holy fuck, that had been amazing.

He leaned up and kissed my shoulder where he'd bitten, the skin already scabbing over. "I love you, Poe Dupin. I'll take care of you and protect you with everything I've got from now until the end of time."

I swallowed the lump in my throat as my eyes became suspiciously wet. Damn. That was . . . sweet. "I love you, too," I mumbled. "And ditto to all that stuff."

Tommy ran the back of his hand over my cheek. "Such a poet."

"Fuck off." I turned my face into the pillow.

He snickered and buried his hand in my hair, massaging my scalp. I must have drifted off because next thing I knew Tommy had turned me onto my back and was washing me with a warm cloth. The heat felt nice. Maybe we could sit in his giant bathtub for a bit? Even though my ass felt surprisingly okay, my leg and arm muscles wouldn't mind some heated relief.

He finished wiping me down, and I opened my mouth to suggest the bath, when he held up a . . . huh? I squinted at it.

Two pieces of metal. One a round ring, the other cylindrical with rings until it came to a rounded tip.

"That had better not be a cock cage." I growled, even using my alpha voice.

He grinned. "It is."

"You expect me to wear that?" I glared.

"I'd like you to."

"And what, you'll keep the key?"

He held up a tiny key that dangled from the end of a necklace. "Mmhmm."

"And if I say no?" The swinging of the key was hypnotic.

"Then I'll respect your request. Though we both know you like the idea of it. You aren't much for someone trying to control your life ... but in bed? You're a completely different birdie, aren't you, sugar?"

No point in lying to him since he could read me like a book. I huffed. I did like the idea. At least to try out. Didn't want to like it, but my dick was sure onboard, trying to rally after the best sex I'd ever had.

"Can we try it, and if I don't like it, you'll remove it?" I asked, breathless.

"Sure, shug, but we both know you're going to love it."

I flipped him off before nodding to give permission. No reason to make it *too* easy.

He placed the ring on first. Having my cock and balls pushed through the ring felt odd but not bad or painful. Tommy added a little lubrication around the metal. Yeah, I really didn't wanna chafe. Then he slid the cage over my dick and snapped the unit together before locking it in place. The sound echoed in the room—or seemed to. I shivered. Having the cage against my skin was a rush, and my traitorous dick tried to get hard. I ran a finger tentatively over the split metal rings.

Tommy watched my face. "You love it."

Heat stole to my cheeks.

"I fucking love it." And didn't that just piss me off.

"Ever had an anal orgasm, birdie?"

"No." Was that even a real thing? My face felt like it was on fire, and my skin itched like it was one size too small. I shifted my hips, and the weight of the cage made me even more aware of it.

"Ever heard a caged bird sing?"

I rolled my eyes. "No."

Tommy smirked. "That's because we're only getting started, sugar."

28

Eight days later, I stood outside the Camden Court Apartments on West Lombard. A modern brick-and-glass building like so many of the structures downtown, the apartments boasted a hexagonal entrance—like a castle turret—on an otherwise "L" shaped layout. Two years ago, management converted half of the top floor into a hot pot restaurant, The Sichuan Tea Room. Considering the hefty price tag and its location in Briggs' Neighborhood, I'd never been. I'd also never had hot pot, though Kennedy raved about it. Without a permanent Roger present, Tommy had easily arranged for me to get a pass into the area so I could have an early dinner with Kennedy.

I still didn't like the idea of spending so much money on a meal, but Tommy reminded me I'd never have to worry about prices again. Still hadn't stuck. Excess might always make me uncomfortable.

Michael insisted on dropping me off in the limo, even called me Alpha Dupin. I wrinkled my nose. Sounded too much like my dad. I was still just Poe, a bird from the wrong side of Baltimore who had one hell of a mate. I grinned, not caring who on the street noticed.

Don't know what I'd done to deserve him, but Tommy was a demon of his word.

The roost continued to settle in, and I wasn't doing too

terrible a job at being alpha. I'd even solved a years-long intrafamily dispute this week. Tommy nudged me in the right direction more than once, and Abe was a huge help.

The twins loved Tommy's penthouse and hadn't put up much fuss when we'd moved in. I promised them it would be our home from now on. Tommy even had their furniture moved from my place into the extra rooms. Turned out he had an eight-bedroom spread. Who knew?

We turned my apartment into my office, while we were rebuilding Spun Gold. Ollie needed a job, and I liked the idea of having a legitimate business. I didn't need to work. Between my roost and Tommy's generosity, I could sit on my ass if I wanted. I'd never been good at stillness. I needed to be in motion. Tommy, of course, could read this and had set a crew to renovate one of the empty shops next to Rumpled Still.

As I approached the door at Camden Courts, a uniformed doorman gave me a dubious look but allowed me to enter. Yeah, still wearing jeans, my leather jacket, and a concert tee. Didn't plan on changing.

I hopped the elevator, punched the fourteenth floor button, and took it to the top. Exiting, I stood in front of glass double doors with the restaurant's name stenciled in large gold lettering. As I reached for the door handle, a hard object jammed against my lower back.

"Don't make a scene, or I'll pull the trigger," a familiar voice spat.

Ethan fucking Short. Just my rotten luck.

"Seriously, Ethan? Don't you have something better to do?"

"Shut the fuck up. You've ruined everything." He pushed me toward a door at the other end of the hall. An emergency exit. "Move."

Should I make a scene? He didn't sound so sane. Would he hurt others? Me, I didn't doubt. A shiver ran along my spine.

Fine. I'd play along. See what he wanted. I shoved down my dread, then pushed through the exit.

"Go up, but don't try anything funny. I've got silver bullets."

I didn't roll my eyes. He might be a cliché, but he could still blow my brains out. Hadn't occurred to me I could be such a liability to Tommy until this moment. Damn it.

I stomped up the stairs, exited onto the roof. A cool evening, the smell of fall leaves overpowering even the odor of exhaust and the mingled food smells from the restaurants in the area. The Bromo Seltzer Tower's clock showed five after the hour. The blond brick tower provided a scenic backdrop to this shitshow. The Steadman Station Firehouse separated the apartments from the tower. From the street, the six fire-engine bays made the buildings look like a giant "U". From up here, I couldn't see the firehouse.

I slowly turned as Ethan leaned against the metal door we'd come through.

"Okay, you got me up here. Now, what do you want?"

He pointed an old Sig Sauer at my head. "Money. Lots of it."

Ethan's hair hung limp, and he had tears in his clothing. His eyes were bloodshot, his skin sallow, and he noticeably trembled. Smelled like he hadn't bathed in days. Withdrawals? Probably. From alcohol or something else, I didn't know. And I didn't really care.

"You're talking to the wrong bird."

"You can get it. Your sugar daddy's rich. Let him give up a little to get his fuck toy back."

Rude.

"What makes you think he'd do it? And, also, are you prepared to face him? You must know he killed Briggs and Susannah Moore. Ate their souls. Gruesome. One out of ten, wouldn't recommend."

"Shut up! You're always talking. Should have beat you down for your mouthiness earlier. We wouldn't be here if I had."

"We wouldn't be here if you had been even a mediocre alpha. You have no one to blame but yourself."

"Fuck you! You don't know what I had to deal with!" His gun hand shook, his finger a little too close to the trigger for my comfort. "I need money. I'm leaving Baltimore."

"Let me guess. Not welcome in Briggs' Neighborhood anymore? MASC not happy with you around?"

His jaw ticked.

Yeah, I'd hit the mark.

"You stole everything from me. My roost, my kids, everything."

"I didn't steal shit. You didn't take care of anyone or anything in your life. You care more about gambling than you do about your kids. They're fine, by the way. Thanks for asking."

His face purpled. May not be a good idea to poke the beast, but he didn't scare me. Much.

"Call your boyfriend and get the money. 100K."

I laughed. "You think he keeps it in his sock drawer?" For all I know, he did, but I wasn't telling Ethan that. "No can do. Best I can offer is to let you walk away and not send him after you."

"You think you're so smart, don't you?" Ethan took a step toward me, the gun still remarkably steady for how much his hand shook.

"In comparison? Yeah."

I stepped into him, moving faster than I thought possible, the power of the roost filling me. I grabbed his wrist.

He pulled the trigger. His shot slid past my shoulder. Could feel the heat on my chin.

I twisted his wrist. Hard.

We both heard the snap as his bones broke.

He howled. Dropped the gun.

I kicked it away but kept ahold of him. Shoved him back against the door. Hard.

"You listen to me, old man, this is the only chance you get. You come near me, the roost, Tommy, or most especially the twins, I'll kill you. We don't owe you anything." The temptation to beat him down made my fingers twitch.

"You can't keep a father away from his kids." He tipped his chin up defiantly.

"You might have been their sperm donor, but you were never their father." I trembled, the urge to close my hands around his neck and squeeze the life out of him becoming a thrum in my veins. With my new alpha strength, I could easily do it, too. I *wasn't* gonna be that kind of alpha. Instead, I released him. "Go."

"I'll make you pay, boy. Mark my words." The dumb fuck dove for the gun. Before he could get it, I kicked it out of reach again. He sprawled in a graceless heap.

"Should have run." I used my alpha voice and drew the strength of the roost around me.

"Stay away from me!" Ethan cowered before all at once shifting into his raven form. He launched himself into the air. He flew straight toward the clock tower and over the edge of the building.

I didn't follow. If he came back, I'd keep my word and kill him, my conscience clear.

Bang!

Shot fired. I ducked.

Ethan squawked. He transformed back into his human form. His arms flailed. He screamed as he fell.

WTF? I spun around in time to see Kennedy pick up a shell casing and toss it in her oversized purse.

"What the hell, Kens?" I gaped at her. "You killed him."

"I'd say gravity did the dirty deed." She shrugged.

"I'm being serious."

"He never would have left you alone, sweetie." She bent and picked up the Sig Sauer and slid it in a pocket in her purse after ejecting the magazine and the bullet in the chamber, then added the Glock. "I highly doubt the acting Roger is going to assign anyone to look into Ethan's unfortunate death."

We stepped to the edge of the roof and looked over. Ethan had plummeted about 11 or 12 stories onto the roof of the fire station. Unnaturally twisted limbs, but I didn't see a puddle of blood or anything. Still, dead as a doornail. No way he survived that fall.

"You shot him. Hard to hide a bullet."

"I *winged* him." She snickered at her joke. Not a hint of remorse.

"I see that." I pinched the bridge of my nose.

"Shug, you okay?" Tommy's voice startled me.

Whoa. "How'd you know to find me up here?"

"I could feel it through our bond. You were . . . distressed. But I see Kennedy handled it nicely." He nodded to her, not looking too pleased.

"Another one you owe me." She grinned.

Tommy glowered. "I would have dealt with him."

I sighed. "You both are so bloodthirsty."

"Thank you," they said in unison.

"And *I* took care of it. I didn't need either of you to help." I scowled.

"We know that. But I utilized a more permanent solution. And this way you don't have to tell the twins *you* killed their father." Kennedy leaned into my shoulder, batted her lashes. "You're not mad at me, are you?"

"No." I wasn't. So she'd killed Ethan. He deserved to die. I'd have to figure out how and when to break the news to the twins. "I wonder how he knew I'd be here?"

"Oh, I let him know." Kennedy straightened up, shrugged. "Anonymously, of course."

Tommy sighed. "Really?"

"What? I was supposed to sit and wait for him to ambush Poe? Tell me you'd handle it differently."

"I'd do it a little less publicly. And I wouldn't use Poe as bait." Tommy stepped to my side, snuggled underneath my arm.

I let him. Turned out, my demon was quite the cuddler.

"Yeah? Well, I'm not dickwhipped." Kennedy looked around. "Pretty evening. Hey, you want to join us for dinner since you took the trouble to come? The hot pot is phenomenal."

Tommy squeezed my waist. "Since I'm here, I suppose I could try it."

"Uh, what about Ethan?" I asked.

"He won't be joining us," Kennedy grinned.

Tommy chuckled.

Yeah, this was my life.

29

"Beautiful."

Well, mostly. I had my arm slung across Tommy's shoulders, and we both stared at my new store. He'd zipped his hoodie, pulled up the hood as if he were cold. The weather did have some bite to it, though it remained sunny.

Even from across the street, I could see Carter and Ollie arguing in front of the plate-glass window of the about-to-be-opened Spun Gold. I adored the sparkly lettering on the sign, the glitter appealing to my raven side. Only two weeks had passed since Ethan's swan dive, yet they'd completed the renovations, added fresh paint, and set up display cases. When Tommy wanted things done, they moved. Quickly.

Ollie busied himself organizing the front window, but Carter clearly didn't agree with his arrangement and kept moving things. They'd become fast friends, though I don't know how Ollie put up with Carter's sass. But I forgave the cat because he always seemed to make Ollie laugh. Not an easy thing to do these days. Though having a hand in Andre's death seemed to give Ollie a certain peace. I could understand that.

However, he wasn't at peace now, if his wild gesturing was any sign.

Boldtalon cawed from the tree behind us. Laughter. Glad he was amused.

Tommy had placed the crow's nest across the street from Spun Gold. The crow already had his avaricious eye on all the shinies in my shop. I'd have to make sure to give him a few pretty but cheaper pieces so he wouldn't be tempted to steal the good stuff.

Kennedy stepped to the window and pointed to the door. Carter threw up his hands and stomped out. He stuck his tongue out at her as he darted back inside the barbershop.

"I think you should send Carter gift-wrapped to Bengal. He's supposed to be irresistible to cats, right? Maybe Carter wouldn't come back." Plus, it would be amusing to see the Rakshasa try to put Carter in line. I grinned thinking about it.

Tommy elbowed me. "You know I'd never do that, sugar. Not only would I lose access to Carter's eyes and ears, but I don't think Baltimore could handle those two together." The glint in Tommy's eye told me he was considering the angles, though.

"Have you heard anything from Garrett?" I tried my best to keep my tone neutral, but I wouldn't fool Tommy.

"I spoke with him this morning. MASC should make their final selections for the new Rogers in a day or two." He didn't say anything else.

Asshole.

"Did he mention Ollie?"

"Now, shug, why would he do that?" Tommy grinned up at me.

"I don't know. You tell me. They seemed to have . . . something, but it's been almost a month and nothing."

"Patience, Poe. There's a season for everything. I had to wait for you."

I snorted. "I was in your bed within a week."

"You were. But it wasn't only your fine body I wanted."

"Aww, who's the poet now?"

Tommy snuggled closer, subtly gripped my hip, letting me know he'd make me pay for the quip later. Couldn't wait.

Now that my shop sat next to his, we'd be spending our lunch hours together. At least when I didn't have roost business. Each day, those duties became more manageable, especially now that Tommy had placed all roost members in jobs fitting their skill sets.

As Kennedy predicted, Ethan's death had been ruled a suicide. It hadn't been easy telling the twins, but luckily they seemed more relieved than heartbroken. That worried me more than anything. Tommy had arranged for them to visit a child therapist once a week, anyway, and we'd have to see how that went.

As we stared at my store, I couldn't help but notice the sign above the barbershop. Rumpled Still: Skin, Hair, and Scalp. I chuckled. Fuck. Me. I knew what the letters on the cube spelled.

"What is it, birdie?" He looked up at me, his brow raised.

"You know, Tommy, it's awfully cheeky of you to name your shop after your true name."

His eyes widened, and then he returned my grin. "Ah, but Poe, the demon's always in the details."

AUTHOR NOTES

When I was a child, my family would make the day-long trek to my grandparents' house every summer. My Aunt Jackie lived with my grandparents, and at bedtime she would tell me a fable. It's one of my fondest memories from my childhood. I would snuggle down in the blankets and she'd pick a different tale than then one she'd told me the night before.

One of my favorite stories remains **Rumpelstiltskin**. I'm not really sure why. The main character is passive through the whole story, and king gets rewarded in the end for being a vile human being (I mean, who threatens to cut off someone's head and then marries them???), and poor Rumpelstiltskin is treated like the villain of the story, when really he's the victim. And yet I love this story. I'd make her tell it over and over again.

So, when Rhys Lawless asked whether I'd be interested in writing an urban fantasy retelling of a fable, I knew instantly I'd choose Rumpelstiltskin . . . because everyone loves a good reclamation story. This was my chance to set the score straight! Instead of a passive main character, I created Poe, a raven shifter who was gutsy and didn't want anyone's help. The "king" would become the equivalent of a mob boss, and my Rumpelstiltskin would become a sexy demon named Tommy, a murder twink who made bargains with terrible people. How hard could this be to write?

Well . . . I'll be honest. It was difficult keeping **The Demon's in the Details** to 60K. I'm not exactly known for short novels, so this proved to be a challenge. I am known, however, for creating plots that weave together many different threads. But my retelling needed to have certain key elements that would mirror the original story. This meant less threads, more focus on finding common elements between the original and my retelling. After much complaining, and a few false starts, I was off and typing.

In the end, I love this story and feel proud of it. I've always been more of a fantasy writer who uses a bit of urban fantasy voice, than an actual urban fantasy writer. So, writing this story made me stretch my wings a little. And I found myself falling in love with Poe and Tommy's story. I like playing with characters who aren't perfect but know how to love fiercely.

Insider Info: I chose the name Poe Dupin because Baltimore is well-known as Edgar Allan Poe's resting place. Dupin comes from one of Poe's most famous characters, C. Auguste Dupin. And it's no coincidence that Poe is a raven shifter. Lots of little tips of the hat to Edgar Allan Poe's genius. And did you know that the story of Rumpelstiltskin was also known by another name? Tom Tit Tot. Hence, Tommy

Tittoti was born. Also, yes, I did select "Roger" as the title for my territory bosses because everyone knows it's Mister Roger's neighborhood.

Thanks for reading! If you enjoyed **The Demon's in the Details**, please consider leaving a review on Amazon, Goodreads, and/or BookBub. Every review helps!

ALSO BY MEGHAN MASLOW

STARFIG INVESTIGATIONS (series)

Book 1 - *By Fairy Means or Foul*: (ebook) (audiobook) (print) (German) (Italian)

Book 2 - *Be Fairy Game*: (ebook) (audiobook) (print) (German) (Italian)

Book 3 - *His Fairy Share*: (ebook) (audiobook) (print)

Book 4 - *Fairy and Impartial*: (ebook) (audiobook) (print)

CHARM CITY CHRONICLES (series)

Book 1 - *The Demon's in the Details*: (ebook) (audiobook) (print) (Italian)

Book 2 - *Cat's Chance in Hell* (ebook) (audiobook) (print)

MUCH ADO ABOUT DEMONS (series)

Short, prequel - *In Fair Verona*: (ebook) (audiobook)

Book .5 - *Demon for the Win*: (ebook) (audiobook) (print)

Book 1 - *Must Love Demons*: (ebook) (audiobook) (print)

Book 2 - *A Demon's Dilemma* (coming soon)

ACKNOWLEDGMENTS

Thank you once again to my amazing writing group: **John Betancourt, Carla Coupe, Karen Diegmueller,** and **Barry Fulton**. You went above and beyond with this one! Thank you for the extra meetings and the quick turn arounds. I literally could not have done this without you all.

Rowan McAllister and **Carla Coupe** deserve huge props for speed-reading in the 11th hour and handholding throughout this project. It's been a doozy of a ride.

A big thank you to **Lauren Weidner.** Another 11th hour save by my ah-mazing editor. Thanks for cleaning up the final details and providing much needed feedback.

Thank you **Andy Gallo** for not choking me out when I'd complain that I hadn't quite found the right voice yet and cheering me on when I finally did. Lol.

Thank you **Rhys Lawless** for inviting me to originally join you and 4 other fantastic UF/PNR authors in the Fables Retold anthology. You helped stretch my writing wings and for that I'm grateful.

Thank you **Alexandria Corza** for the great cover! You do great work!

Finally, thank you to my family. **Mister Maslow,** once again you went on countless walks where I would pour out my latest sticking points. And you weathered my foul moods when the words weren't coming. Thank you to my **kids** who've been so patient with me this year and have given lots of hugs and encouragement. Also, a thank you to my **parents** for coming to visit the day after I needed to have this draft turned in, lol. With everything going on in the world, I so needed a week off to enjoy family time with you. Knowing you'd be on my doorstep was the extra push I needed to get across the finish line. I wasn't willing to miss a single minute of your visit. Talk about motivation!

ABOUT THE AUTHOR

Mischief, Magic, and Murder... That's a Maslow!
If you're looking for comedy, fantasy, or dead bodies in your romances—sometimes all three at once!—I'm your gal.

I'm also a. . . *gasp!*. . . extroverted writer. It seems counterintuitive that as someone who is energized by people, I spend most of my time alone. Yet, that's the case. And I don't mind.

Mostly.

If I get writer's block or start to go a little stir crazy, I head out to a coffee shop, a restaurant, a friend's place—anywhere to fill up my need for human contact. It also helps that I spend a lot of time with the voices in my head. Some of them are really quite opinionated.

I love writing gay romance because I'm a sap for a happy ending, and I believe everyone—regardless of orientation—should be able to find books that have them. And if that romance comes with a dash of **mischief**, **magic**, or **murder**, all the better.

I believe that life is for living, kindness is contagious, and a good book makes the world a better place.

Printed in Great Britain
by Amazon